W9-BWT-135

FINALLY, THE *OTHER* SIDE OF THE APOCALYPSE STORY

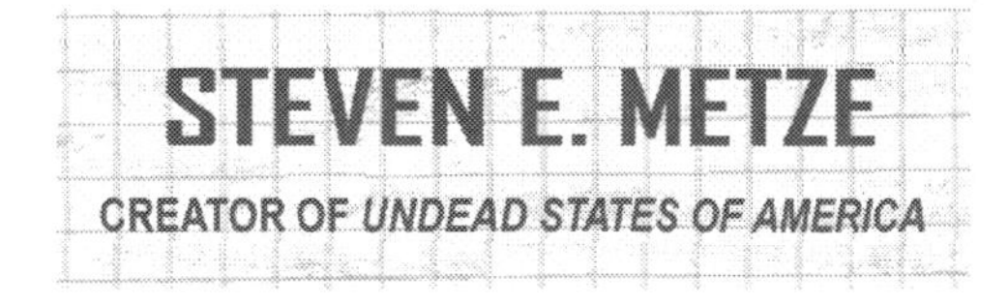

This is a work of fiction. All of the characters, organizations, and events portrayed in this novel are either products of the author's imagination or are used fictitiously. Any resemblance to actual persons, living, dead or undead, events, or locales, is entirely coincidental.

DRAGONFIRE PRESS

Dragonfire Press is a dba of Scum Crew Pictures LLC

Printed in the United States of America.

www.zombiemonologues.com

www.ubergoobergames.com

ISBN 978-0-615-49603-0

First Paperback Edition

10 9 8 7 6 5 4 3 2 1

For Alwynne

who inspires me daily to go forth and do great things

ACKNOWLEDGEMENTS

Thanks to my Wife and her endless patience and encouragement

Thanks to my parents and my sister and their boundless support

Thanks to Ramona, Carol, Cory, Phaidra and Laurie for their insightful thoughts and commentary

Thanks to the All Things Writing group for regular inspiration and wisdom

Thanks to CMM for talking to me about psychology and anything else that popped into his head. R.I.P.

Thanks to Papa Elliott for keeping me honest. R.I.P.

Thanks to Cedrick just because

Thanks to Max Brooks for bringing the Z War to the World

And a very special thanks to Paul, Patrick and Eric for the macabre sense of humor which got this whole thing started

123TH CONGRESS
5TH SESSION

INTERIM SENATE

DOCUMENT
123-5

INVESTIGATION OF THE NAD PSYCHOLOGICAL LABORATORY FACILITY IN RELATION TO THE GREAT ZOMBIE WAR

THE EVIDENTIARY RECORD PURSUANT TO INTERIM SENATE RESOLUTION 257

VOLUME XXIII

Hearing of the Interim Subcommittee "Background and History of the Great Zombie War"

Printed at the direction of Michael Kawalski, Secretary of the Interim Senate, pursuant To I.S. Res. 257, 123rd Cong., 5th Sess.

Ordered to be printed

U.S. GOVERNMENT PRINTING OFFICE
ALASKA

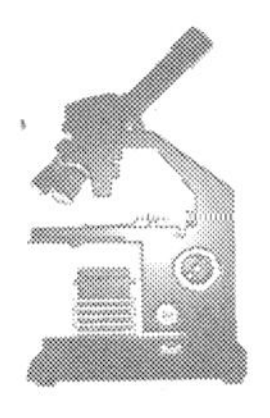

FORWARD

(Taken from Resident Eve Langley's Personal Journal)

Sitting on a military helicopter next to three struggling corpses, I'm more nervous about my first day working with Dr. Marshall than the masses howling and grasping up from 1000 feet below.

The great northeastern horde. From up here they could easily be mistaken for one of those giant herds in documentaries about the Serengeti. They cover every piece of flat ground from one horizon to the other, kicking up dust as they scramble after the sounds of the rotor blades. It's sort of hypnotic though, watching them move as a group. Their ambling motions give the whole thing the rhythm of slow waves in a filthy red-black sea.

Soon we'll be rising up over the foothills of the Appalachians on our way to Columbus Ohio with the last three of our ten experimental subjects. We finally found a married couple, so that will be interesting, although not nearly as exciting as subject Sigourney. After four months of phone calls, promises and bribes, Dr. Marshall should be returning with her body back from England some time later tonight. Whatever we find out about her I'm confident will validate the NAD facility three times over.

Meanwhile, a couple of slabs to my right, I think the undead soldier is making the hired guns a little edgy. Probably because they're all wearing the same outfit. No one likes to look down and be reminded of how much they have in common with something like... like that. I admit it is sort of terrifying, sitting next to three squirming bodies, but regardless, I'm still more nervous about tomorrow.

In my defense, I've been waiting for this moment since NAD hit the public consciousness. Although, obviously back then no one called it "Necrotizing Ambulation Disorder." The media named it Athena's Disease, which I guess made sense. I mean, when a world-renowned actress super-model pop-singer and anti-poverty activist suddenly transitioned to NAD Stage 2 in the middle of the Academy Awards, well, that had an effect. I think everyone remembers where they were that night, even if they weren't watching. Least we could do was name the plague in her honor. I certainly would have wanted it that way if it had been me.

Even though this is a personal journal entry, if I'm going to be the Project Historian as part of my residency, I should get used to adding in all the little details for the formal documents. I'm Ph.D. Resident Eve Langley, and I'm a 37-year-old just starting my third year of residency in mental health with a focus on abnormal psychology. Both my parents and my only sibling were in a neighborhood overrun by zombies my senior year at med school. I never learned if they were entirely consumed, escaped, or turned, although the news reported an Air Force strike in the area shortly thereafter. After graduation I had nowhere else to go, so based on rumors of his research, I applied to work under Dr. Marshall, and he chose me over 12 other applicants. While I doubt I'll ever find my parents or my brother, if there somehow is a chance anything survived of my family, at least mentally, Dr. Marshall was the only one trying to discover how to get to it.

Dr. Marshall claimed it was beyond his scope to discuss the philosophical ramifications of NAD, and referred the interested student to the papal encyclical *Malleus Mortuos Viventes* or Dr. Jonas Goodfellow's *Chicken Soup for the Zombie Soul.* However, the mechanics of the undead mind – the once highly developed cerebellum transformed into little more than a carnivorous mobile plant – that was something he simply couldn't let go unexplored. After a few months of neurological research, he theorized early on that the Athena virus didn't destroy brain tissue as quickly as everyone assumed. He proposed that the original person remained in there, and we owed it to society to let them out. Using the words from his first grant proposal, his goal was "to free them from that hellish captivity."

Dr. Marshall believed that the topic of the NAD Experience was held as taboo in general conversation and most forms of literature for far too long. In his notes, he wrote that to hide the accounts of these "zombies" would warp what has really gone on within the millions of people world-wide who have otherwise become comedic caricatures of mindless cannibalistic fiends.

And I really believe our work is going to leave everything done before it behind. (I like that I get to say "our" work now.) While Dr. Marshall was personally retrieving subject Sigourney from a holding facility in Wales, PhD Resident Zach Smithee (more on him later) and I were performing a sequence of neural decoding tests that Dr. Marshall left for us. He theorized that the diseased brains did not decay right away, and founded the facility in the hopes of gaining a better understanding of the post-necrotic but ***active*** brain, and of improving communications with the "undead" who could no longer speak or write. To sum up, we set out to actually see the memories of these tortured individuals.

After mapping brain activity in normal, healthy human brains, Zach and I were able to modify the recognized patterns to compare with the lower brain activity of the recently undead. Our first attempts retrieved visual video footage of colors and swirling patterns which occasionally took a recognizable shape. After another two months of comparison mapping, we were able to retrieve thought patterns and decode them into actual words. Tomorrow we start our interviews, which I believe will provide valuable insight as to how we came to be in this thing everyone refuses to call a war.

I'll be in charge of the primary cataloguing, and Dr. Marshall sent me a long email about entrusting me with the manuscript. In addition to capturing everything with scientific validity, he encouraged me to compose something forthright that would prepare the average layman for the NAD Experience. He wanted something that would leave it up to the audience to draw their own conclusions. The only text Dr. Marshall provided to me was something he wanted to make sure got added to the final document:

"To condemn this material is to condemn the true authors, the many undead whom I subjected to hours of brain scanning and verbal interviews. They are the real storytellers. I only kept the record."

Psychological Studies on the Necrotizing Ambulation Disorder (NAD) Experience

The Zombie Monologues - Volume I

"The *other* side of the Apocalypse story."

A documentary of "undead" memories and conversations collected through neural decoding and memory pattern-detection software.

By Clyde Marshall, Ph.D.

Consulting and Counseling Neurologist/Psychologist

Compiled by Ph.D. Resident Eve Langley and Ph.D. Resident Zachariah Smithee

A list and brief description of the nine primary subjects, all names changed to protect their identities.

1. ***Tom – High School Student***
2. ***Lisa – College student***
3. ***Ricky – Corporate executive***
4. ***Sam and Janis – Performing couple (stand-up comedy venue)***
5. ***Sigourney – Journalist and author***
6. ***Marie – Religious activist***
7. ***Richelle – Molecular biologist***
8. ***Dead Eddie – Soldier***
9. ***Jonathan – Political activist***

Day 1

Case Study "Tom"

(Resident Eve Notes: Subject "TOM" is a 17-year-old deceased white male in Stage 2 of Necrotizing Ambulation Disorder. He is the first subject after the initial trials to map out the English language from brain signals to typed words. We began the interview by inputting the phrase "Tell beginning" near the subject's hippocampus, about 2cm above the base of the brain stem.)

I didn't realize what had happened at first. I'd bandaged the bite and poured a whole bottle of rubbing alcohol on it like two days before, so I figured I was okay. I mean, it seemed to make sense, and I felt fine. Well, my vision was a little blurry, and the idea of eating vegetables made my stomach churn, but that was it.

Me and my girlfriend and some of my other buddies had headed down to join the riots – not because we wanted to be part of a cause. We didn't even know what started it. We were just hoping to grab some free loot.

I mean, why not? All the stores were going to claim all the damage on their insurance, anyway. It was either let it burn or put it to good use. That seemed like an easy choice to me.

I guess that makes us criminals. But dude, I think by then everyone had broken one law or another. I know my dad buried a stash of cans of soup and shotgun shells out in the backyard when the food and ammo census came by. And don't think he didn't think about trying to get a free gun out of the deal. In that first pass, they were passing out shotguns and pistols to anybody who held out their hand.

Well, except kids, which I never understood. Instead they gave us classes on symptoms and, get this, how to tell if we needed to shoot our own parents. "An unpleasant topic," they said, "but something you must be prepared to do." Actually I guess that does explain why they didn't give us guns. Not right after they gave us permission to take out our own folks.

My dad stayed so focused on defending the house, filling sandbags, welding bars up everywhere, I don't even know if he knew I left. It was totally safe, at least in our neighborhood, and I only did it because he made such a big deal about how I shouldn't. Besides, if I let my girlfriend go out alone in something like that with my other friends, she was going to come back as somebody else's girlfriend.

Once we hooked up, we all wandered the streets for a couple of days, camping out in abandoned stores, using clothes for pillows, and scrounging food off restaurant shelves and smashed up convenience stores. Early on we passed through a big crowd and I came out of it with a chunk taken out of my forearm. Didn't see who did it. Didn't care. Figured one small wound in exchange for one of those… ***(Resident Eve Notes: At this point Tom visualizes a large flat screen TV, but the word he associates with it is unintelligible.)*** would be well worth it.

Maybe I should have paid more attention to the symptoms. Maybe any of us should have. I just thought I had really bad gas. Now that I really think about it, I think my girlfriend knew. I mean, not that I had bad gas – she always knew that – I think that she understood it was something worse.

She got more and more touch-crabby after that. First she didn't want to be kissed, then she didn't even want my arm around her. I was totally pissed at first, but at the same time she said these really sweet things to me. Like how she really liked me and how much she liked my smile, the sort of thing you tell someone you aren't ever planning on seeing again, I guess.

Then one afternoon I took a nap, and when I woke up everyone else was gone. I remember it seemed much harder to get up than usual, and for some reason doorknobs completely confused me. I don't know how much time passed, but I must have spent hours just staring at this one door, absolutely fascinated by it. I still can't recall exactly how the damn things work, but now whenever I think of one, I get really angry. Like, I just want to stand and stare at it angry. That sort of angry.

There were some sounds then, I guess from outside. It seemed like I needed to head towards them, so I did. Eventually I did find a door somebody left open, and made it out into the street.

It was crazy. People were totally freaked out and running and screaming all over the place for some bizarre reason. I gently took one older lady by the wrist to ask what was so horrifying, but she fainted when her arm came off. I took a few minutes to pop open her forehead and scoop out a few mouthfuls of brains and then tried to flag down a policeman. I never found one.

(Resident Eve Notes: A fast-cut series of riot images flew by next, with no words describing them. This continued for two hours, only slowing to real time whenever Tom physically made contact with someone, which was fatal for the person contacted three out of seven times. In all cases Tom treated the mauling as accidental. This continued until we prompted him again with "When did you realize?")

Realize what?

(Resident Eve Notes: We repeated the question and got no response. Since Tom had long lost his ability to use his eyes, we inserted an image of his current face into the brain feed. That too produced no result. Then we inserted an image that the DMV had on file, after we digitally blended it with his present image.)

Oh *that*. Well, it was different than I expected. The whole thing was different. After a while I started to comprehend that I didn't recognize most of the people I was hanging out with. It was sort of like waiting in a really long line, or a crowded concert, all the time. You just moved where everyone else moved. And that seemed to make sense.

I think the first thing that started to tip me off was when we wandered through some building after some kids who were running from us – probably some sort of game. They were cool little dudes. Then I stumbled and fell into the door of a restroom. It flew open and I lost my balance and staggered inside.

(Resident Eve Notes: Tom pauses for six and a half minutes until we prompt "Go on.")

So, I remembered it was a restroom, and I knew I was supposed to do something there. Like, it felt like a really familiar place, but I couldn't figure out what to do.

There was this man, well, most of a man, lying on the floor behind one of the other littler doors, and I went over and asked him if he knew. It took me longer than usual to get the words out, but I'm sure I got it right.

Nothing. He didn't say anything.

Man, that sort of thing is annoying, you know?

Finally I heard that noise again, a distant scream, and then I was craving something to eat like you couldn't imagine. I stood up and saw another guy was in the room with me, looking right into my eyes. I asked him if he knew and he didn't say anything either. So then I got really angry. Like, I just wanted to stand and stare at him angry. That sort of angry. And I did. For about a week, I think. And you know, a week didn't seem like a long time to be angry like that, either. There were no distractions, no movement or loud noises to pull me away. It seemed very peaceful, for angry, I mean.

Then finally I noticed that he… oh, this is really embarrassing.

(Resident Eve Notes: After another three minutes, "Go on.")

So, it finally dawned on me that I was looking into a mirror, okay? I had all these, you know, bumps, and holes, and cuts, and well, there were parts showing that I'm pretty sure weren't supposed to be showing.

Oh, I don't mean my dork. I mean, you know, stuff that should be on the inside. Not my dork. That wasn't hanging out. My insides.

(Resident Eve Notes: Tom repeated variations on this sentence for another seven minutes, "And?")

So that's when I knew. You know.

(Resident Eve Notes: Although a lot of the specific text was decoded after the interview had concluded, Tom was our first successful "conversation" beyond just a handful of one-syllable words. Following this breakthrough, we were able to use the computer to input images or typed messages, or to speak directly into a microphone and have our words recoded and implanted directly into the subject's brain. This microphone-speech method led to much more fluid conversations from that point forward.)

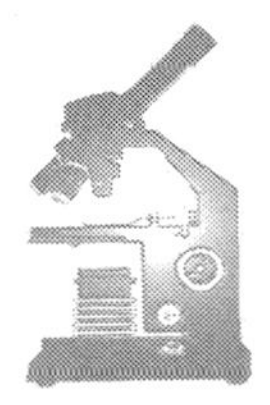

Day 2

Equipment Calibration Test

(Resident Eve Notes: Zach wanted to test out system that would mix simple words with complex emotions and combine both into more advanced vocabulary for our subjects. He interviewed me using a version of the equipment fashioned from external contacts in order to help recalibrate the system. I included some parts of the transcript here that provided useful information.)

Resident Z: "Let's start with something easy."

Like what?

Resident Z: "I don't know. Talk about something you know."

Like… what?

Resident Z: "I need it to start with something you're familiar with. Talk about yourself I guess."

Seriously?

Resident Z: "Yes, seriously."

Right. Hispanic female. Age and weight none of your business. Medium length brown hair that I keep down anywhere I go except for the cleanroom, where I wear it up in a bun.

Resident Z: "OK, now try something harder."

You have to give me more to go on than that.

Resident Z: "Let's try you turning around and describing me for a memory test. Be honest so I get a good base line reading."

If you say so.

(Resident Eve Notes: I turned and closed my eyes, concentrating on picturing what he looked like)

Last week I met the only other Ph.D. Resident at the facility, Zachariah Smithee. Zach is a 35-year-old white male who still insists on a rather long and, if I may say so, unkempt beard, but wears a special mask for it in the cleanroom, so Dr. Marshall allows it. From what I've gathered, Zach was raised in an Amish community before quitting that to pursue a life of science. While he claims he too has a keen interest in zombie mental processes, at times he also seems acutely aware of what this research could mean for his career. However, since Zach is a genius in both computer science and neurology, Dr. Marshall could hardly turn him down.

(Resident Eve Notes: He paused a few seconds longer than was needed to adjust the equipment before responding)

Resident Z: "That might have been a little too much honesty."

Just trying to be a good subject here.

Resident Z: "Let's go something easier. Describe Dr. Marshall instead."

Describing my boss is easier?

Resident Z: "Should be. You're a therapist type. Don't you guys love direct conversation?"

If he were here, this would be a direct conversation, although hardly a productive one.

Resident Z: "Look, you like the mental stuff, I like making things work."

Fine, describing my boss. What all do I know about my boss… ?

Let's see. As for Dr. Marshall himself, he is the founder of the NAD Psychological Laboratory Facility just outside Columbus Ohio. If I remember correctly, he's 58-years-old, and of Scottish and maybe Italian decent. Little over six feet tall, with dark hair, and very blue eyes. Also the pasty complexion one would expect from some-one who rarely leaves the lab during daylight hours. While we were discussing clean room etiquette he claimed that he was hairier than most men, although he maintains a clean shave so that should he ever need to don a protective mask it will seal properly against his face. I'm pretty sure he started as a neurologist, then went back and got a degree in psychology, specializing in behavior disorders linked with violence and socially deviant behavior. His interest in zombies, ac-cording to him, also began the instant he saw the footage of that now infamous final Academy Awards episode.

Resident Z: "Is that it?"

That's all you're getting.

Resident Z: "I need more."

Do I have to describe a person?

Resident Z: "Just needs to be from memory is all."

I'll talk about the lab then.

Resident Z: "Whatever. That works. Just keep your eyes closed and keep talking."

Let's go with the primary lab, a level ten clean room. For those of you at home, level ten means it has a very low level of dust and, most importantly, airborne microbes. The air is filtered and then constantly re-circulated through super low particulate air filters to remove contaminants. Everyone entering or leaving wears special gowns, face masks, and gloves, plus booties over our shoes. The door is an airlock with special sticky paper on the floor to pick up anything off the bottom of the booties as we come in or out of the airlock. This may sound like we are being overly zealous, but if you were dealing with some of the stuff we were dealing with, you'd want even more secure if you could get it.

Resident Z: "Keep going."

What else?

Oh, the room is 20 feet by 30 feet, with one whole wall covered with sealed chambers containing the remains of most of our subjects. We use full-body chambers to store our cadavers, different from the common practice in other facilities of removing their heads for study purposes and disposing of the primary torso. In all cases, our subjects are brought out into the primary examination table where the scanning equipment is attached. The heads are set into a vise-like apparatus and their eyes are blindfolded to keep them from moving or attempting to bite the hands of the attendants moving them into position.

The scanner appears like a basic computer with three flat screens hooked up in a basic array of wires, plugs, and tubes, all attached to the outside of or feeding into the subject's head. Obviously in my case, we went with the outside of the head version.

Is that enough yet?

Resident Z: "Almost. Go with something really abstract, like what we were talking about this morning."

Can you narrow it down for me?

Resident Z: "The new stages thing."

Oh that, right.

While anyone who has taken junior high health class understands the five basic steps of Stage 1 of Athena's Disease, with Tom as a model, we also began classifying the progression of NAD beyond clinical body death. Most of our subjects from this point forward were of the Stage 2 variety (i.e., newly dead). They proved to be the most recently 'turned' – all less than a year, and less than six months in most cases – and those who showed the least brain deterioration or damage. We anticipate carrying this all the way to what we suspect will be successful, albeit hostile, Stage 3 interviews, but probably none with any subjects after they progress to the bestial Stage 4. We theorize at this point that Stage 4 interviews may never be possible, given the extreme damage done to the higher brain functions.

Resident Z: "Got it. It's a wrap."

Do I get to interview you next?

Resident Z: "I'm going to bed. See you in the morning."

(Resident Eve Notes: He turned off his part of the equipment, but left me with all the rest still attached to my head without saying another word. I suspect that despite my MD, he still believes my science to be 'softer' than his. We'll see.)

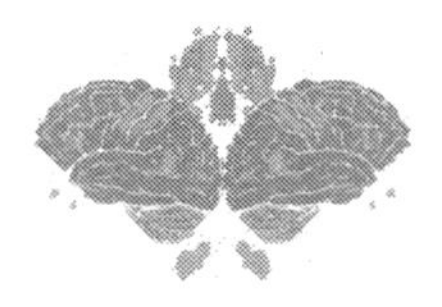

Day 6

Case Study "Sigourney"

Interview #1

(Resident Eve Notes: When you examine everything out there, I think Dr. Marshall only had two real rivals in the field. One was some authority on Nonliving Anthropology whose name I can't remember, although I do recall he was the author of the well-known treatise, "*Group consumption rituals by reanimated surrogate kinship groups.*" The other - when she was alive – was someone whose work was truly groundbreaking.

Subject "SIGOURNEY" is a 34-year-old deceased black female international journalist in NAD Stage 2. Sigourney is one of the two "protected" subjects we have in the lab, primarily because of her notoriety and celebrity status. She is dark skinned, with shoulder length dreadlocks. She has a number of very dark specks on her cheeks, giving her slightly plump face a youthful hue to it, despite its morbid condition. Other than a few still-open small caliber bullet wounds in the left side of her torso, she is otherwise free of overt external trauma.

Because the date of her "turning" is well documented, we know that Sigourney is one of our oldest functioning samples still at NAD Stage 2, approaching the one year mark. For this

reason, plus her extensive knowledge on the topic of zombies, Sigourney will be one of our more exhaustive and reoccurring interviews. She is best known for her work,* Undead Like Me, *a best-selling account of her time disguised and living with the great northeastern zombie hordes. She was bitten and infected, ironically, not as part of her research, but in a small town in Wales on the European book tour promoting her work. We began the interview by implanting an image of her book cover.)

It's a question I asked myself every time I watched one of the old zombie fiction movies: Why don't zombies attack each other? It seemed like a simple concept. Zombies like human flesh, they are human flesh, ergo, why don't they take a bite out of that slow moving fellow to their immediate left instead of spending hours trying to catch up with someone more fleet of foot? And for that matter, the argument goes that zombies are unbelievably stupid, so even if there was some reason why they wouldn't go after other zombies, how could they tell us from them? Or, I guess now, us from you.

First off, we weren't scientists. I came up with the idea and proposed it to my editor, and he gave me a "budget" only in the sense that it involved money on paper. Really it was an advance, all out of my paycheck if I didn't come back with something that paid back a hundred times that. I didn't tell the rest of the team that part. Although, I guess that didn't matter too much since only two of my team were on the payroll and the other six were interns. Hard to imagine an organization that gives out a billion a year in bonuses alone couldn't come up with thirty or even twenty grand to toss at an idea as original – and dangerous – as this one. I think he knew it was brilliant, but just wanted to be an ass about it. That's what execs do, even when they don't have to. If I failed, I'd be dead, and he could just pass the idea on to someone else with some star-power behind them.

I'm not sure, but I think it must have taken nearly five weeks to get permission to enter one of the holding pens. I lost my first intern over the paperwork alone. I guess the holding facilities had a lot of trouble with the Undead Heads and the Zactivists and didn't want to let anyone in without official business. Maybe it was easier to keep everyone out and so they devised an approval process so complex, so Machiavellian in its deviousness, it turned away anyone whose entire journalistic career wasn't riding on that one stamp of approval. Like it was for me.

When we finally got it, we started simple. First we attached collars to all the zombies using nooses, sort of like the kind they use to catch dogs. Each collar we hooked to a chain that we'd measured out so none of the zeds could get to the back ten feet of the pen. They could go anywhere else, but not there.

Then we made a noise near the front of the pen, and they all headed towards it, surprise. While they were distracted, we snuck Dave in the back wearing torn bloody clothing. We told him to just stand there and see if they noticed.

Well, they did, almost right away. He even tried limping around a little bit but that just attracted more of them. Our first thought was that the blood on Dave's shirt was too fresh, so we let it get dry and crusty and tried it again. Same thing.

We ran through all sorts of variations after that. Dave in zombie make-up, we brought in this new age alternative ballet troupe who teach zombie interpretive dance (don't ask) and talked them into giving Dave special zombie movement classes – he hated those – we even planted a little speaker on him that gave off a continuous zombie moan. All failed.

We took a step back at that point and went with just bowls of blood. We used old zombie blood, fresh zombie blood, the blood of an infected but still living person, and normal blood. Without exception, every zombie went after the normal blood, and wouldn't touch any of the rest. Well, there was one exception. Our first breakthrough came with a young male zombie we called Nosy, because his entire nose and nasal passages were missing. We were clever that way. Anyway, he actually went through tasting each variant before settling on the normal blood. This told us that zombies could detect each other both through smell AND taste. It was a major breakthrough, although we kept all our findings secret. We, and by we I mean I, didn't want anything to leak out before we were ready to publish.

The next week we put Dave out there again, but this time every time he went out with different scents on him. Perfumes, after-shaves, rotten vegetables, spoiled milk, bad eggs, zombie blood, fecal matter… it was actually a pretty good time dumping all that stuff on him. He quit after about two days, naturally, and so after a week of training we got another intern named Madhu to go in next.

Madhu resisted it slightly less, but the results were the same until we finally tried smearing him with the blood of infected humans who hadn't turned. On Day 13, it worked. He stood there and he seemed invisible, at least until he smiled, and then they rushed his direction.

Okay, got it, displays of emotions triggered them, too. We hadn't anticipated that more than one stimulus could trigger their feeding response, and now we had three: Scent, taste, and visual cues.

On Day 15 Madhu went an hour standing around before any of them noticed. Then he got cocky and moved in to see how close he could get. He had the drag-leg shuffle, he had the scent, he had the torn clothing, he had the blank stare. Everything worked perfectly until I thought he was getting too close and called him back. He refused. So I called him back again, and he continued to play the role. The third time he got angry, and one second too late he realized during that instant his face contorted in frustration.

Oh, God, that… that was…

(Resident Eve Notes: A series of horrific mutilation images popped up here from an exterior point of view of a crowd swarming an individual in their midst. Mostly of the standard red mist and occasional disassociated limb flying through the air variety. Not to sound callus, but I'm assuming everyone has seen at least one of those. The image fluttered a few times, and

my interpretation of the signal was of Sigourney trying to stop the flashback. If that was her intention, then overall her attempt failed. She didn't begin talking again until the entire scene played out)

When they were done with him there wasn't enough left to turn. It was my fault, and I took full responsibility for his death in my book. But his passing meant something. He taught us, he taught me, what I needed to do to walk among them undetected.

(Resident Eve Notes: Sigourney became quite a reserve for us for insights into the rest of our research. For many of the first few interviews we simply collected data from her. It would be weeks later before we realized she was doing all the giving, and we weren't returning anything. A classic mistake from scientists and other professionals, latching on to new sources of information or work resources, relentlessly mining them for all they are worth, without realizing that they are living, or unliving creatures. As Dr. Marshall put it, "There is no excuse for such behavior, only explanation and attempts at redemption." You will see in later interviews that we began shifting our sessions into something less of an interrogation and more therapeutic.)

Day 13

Case Study "Ricky"

Interview #1

(Resident Eve Notes: Subject "RICKY" is a 45-year-old deceased white male in NAD Stage 2. Thanks to a rather sizeable amount of legal representation, Ricky is the other of the two "protected" specimens we keep in the lab. There are, to date, 15 court orders demanding everything from body preservation to periodic medical inspections from private medical teams. We're giving them technical notes on the experiments, but not any of the transcripts or any indication that we can actually communicate with the deceased. They can find that out when we're published, just like everyone else. Ricky is a tall, skeletal man now, just as I suspect he was while living. His hair is sandy blonde and cut in a juvenile fashion that makes me wonder how he was ever hired by a corporation in the first place. As a component of one of the court orders, he remains in a suit at all times, in this case a charcoal pin-stripe with a bright red tie. This outfit not only gives him more of a funeral-corpse appearance, but also conceals the various shrapnel wounds to his abdomen and legs. We began the interview with "Tell us about yourself")

I was a band geek in high school, but I knew someday I was going to be the top of the ladder. And I was, too. I still am, really, just a different ladder.

I did internships during my undergrad at some of the pharmaceutical corporations in town. Easier to get near the big guys if they don't have to worry about paying or promoting you. Bounced around a bit, got my name out there, then vanished long enough to get my MBA and come back to where I was familiar, but not too familiar.

I hopped on the corporate fast track early. A few choice successes, a few quarters doing the impossible, and I jumped from manager to director faster than anyone in the drug trade – well, legal drug trade – since the seventies. Then I did a little job hopping – each time a little bit higher pay and position – and there was no stopping me. Finally I realized that the Undead Industry was a growth market, and I moved over to New Biotech.

They were ripe for change. Actually, every corporation is ripe for change, always. It's just a matter of finding what needs to be changed and focusing attention your way at the moment someone flips a switch or at the moment some metric spikes up ridiculously high.

In this case, one of the first things I did was meet with our lobbyists and review all their plans for getting Congress to allow more zombie testing. They had general guidance, fairly good direction, but no real weight behind them. We shifted focus a little bit, and while no one law ever made it through, plenty of special amendments to other unrelated laws sure did. Really, with those amendments, we pioneered zombies as a resource.

After that, streamlining production went much faster. But what really sealed the deal, the real feather in my cap, was when I presented my idea for the PR campaign and our cosmetics line. Get this: "If it works on *them*, it will work on anybody."

(Resident Eve Notes: The software decoded approximately twenty seconds of laughter here)

You couldn't come right out and say it that way, of course. No one was going to stand someone comparing them to a corpse. No, you had to just imply it. "Zombie tested, mother approved," or something like that. Oh God, it was brilliant. In the stores, no difference, but Internet and telephone mail order sales – you know, the places where people could buy stuff with no one seeing them buy it – they were up 30% the first quarter we implemented that plan, and 42% the quarter after. We were able to cut down our employee burden in the shops while increasing our margin in the warehouses. That landed me in the role of VP of Operations.

Dr. M: "It sounds like things worked very well for you."

Unfortunately, like all great leaders, I attracted my fair share of enemies. The standard office variety adversaries were no big deal. I made sure they were the first to go during any downturns, and since I usually had a pretty good idea when those downturns were coming, I was able to leverage their departures to my advantage. Now Vice President Dudley, my peer, he always hated me. Clearly one of us would be CEO one day, and we both knew it. For the most part though, we kept each other in check. Dudley and I never let the other one attend a meeting without being there to defend ourselves and our plans. A true balance of power act.

No, the big problems came from the Zed-huggers. Some religious fliers about some network our parent corporation also owned broadcasting pro-zombie propaganda, then a letter complaining here, a formal complaint there, then a group of them showed up in the office with video cameras demanding an interview, which of course we ignored. Then protests, and more protests, then some minor and distracting lawsuits. I don't think they understood we commanded practically a battalion of lawyers. They never had a chance and never will. Not on that front.

Then one of the little punks disguised herself as a delivery girl and snuck some zombie blood into our water supply. Gotta admire it on some level. Hell, I never met her or saw whoever did it, but if I hadn't been one of the targets, I'd have hired her on the spot as soon as I heard about it. Probably made her a director, too. Just wish I'd thought of it first.

Dr. M: "I'm assuming you consumed some of the tainted water then?"

I've always been a thin guy, not really tan, and, well, I'm embarrassed to say that after I changed, people didn't notice at first. Or at least they didn't say anything if they did. The standard working level grunts weren't big on the whole "Sir, you tie is on crooked," or "You have a stain on your pants" or "Your skin has gone cold and you're leaking pus out of both ears" school of commentary. Too spineless, all of them. Heh, especially that one clerk I got on the way out. But that's jumping ahead.

Bottom line, I thought I was fine, just some minor gastrointestinal distress issues, and went to the Friday morning board meeting like nothing was wrong.

In retrospect, I did think it was odd that the catered hors d'oeuvres were modeled after the CFO's upper torso. At least I got a bite out of Dudley before he made it out of the room.

(Resident Eve Notes: Almost a minute of laughter decoded here)

I'm not afraid to say I'm a zombie now. And let's face it, we're here to stay, and we're expanding. We had excellent results last quarter, and I don't see us slowing down any time soon. We'll have to take a look at our overall organization and how it is laid out, but I think we can capture a lot more of the biological market share next year.

Unfortunately, this restructuring means some of our colleagues' lives are negatively impacted. These decisions are never easy and require all of us to go through difficult periods of transition. I can only ask that you continue to have empathy for those who experience sudden breathing loss and that you enable yourselves and your global team members to embark on our journey to "The *Potential* America."

(Resident Eve Notes: The three of us got together and discussed our thoughts on Ricky. My opinion is that this episode is illustrative of Ricky's abuse of power as perhaps a mechanism to all his self-justification for participation in mass murder activities he probably wouldn't have done otherwise. After the formal interview, Dr. Marshall allowed me to ask Ricky to list incidents he could recall where he engaged in group manslaughter activity when he was alive. He could not list or remember any event where he followed through with any desire to eat the entrails of anyone before he became a zombie. At the time I considered this a meaningful therapy "turning point." I foolishly thought, or perhaps just hoped, that he began to accept the connection between his death and his desire for living flesh, and that had he still been alive, he would not think eating others to be okay.)

Day 16

(Resident Eve Notes: Once we get the calibration right for each subject, the interviews so far have gone fairly smoothly. However, we've experienced numerous delays during this period while we do the initial tests and load it all in the computers. This has led to several late nights alone with the subjects in the main clean room.

Up close they're nothing resembling that sight I saw from the helicopter window. They aren't just pale people with random spots of blood and torn clothing either. They have big chucks of torn flesh hanging loose like slabs of cold jagged rubber, and their faces almost all have something really wrong with them. Swollen lips, smashed cheeks, crushed in jaw like this guy strapped across the bench next to me. I think we as a species just can't handle something that asymmetrical, or that flawed with the human face.

I can tell it affects several of the others here at the facility, being in such close quarters with the virus and its victims. Knowing that – lurid portrayals of the media not withstanding – NAD is actually a particularly virulent form of Prion disease similar to Kuru doesn't do much to put anyone at ease.

Dr. Marshall keeps a humble staff at the labs, consisting of a day shift of approximately ten full-time employees, plus half that for an early evening shift, along with a handful of graduate students. Almost everyone who works here has been affected, one way or another, by someone with NAD. Despite all this, however, there is still an overwhelming feeling, nurtured by Dr. Marshall's energy and passion for the topic, that the people of this institution will make a significant difference to the future of this world through our research in post-necrotic communications.)

Day 22

Case Study "Lisa"

(Resident Eve Notes: Subject "LISA" is a 21-year-old deceased Lebanese female in NAD Stage 2 who had been a student at Rutgers University. Lisa's hair was originally long and curly, although a significant portion of it has been pulled out, violently from the looks of it, from the right rear portion of her skull. Besides two bullet holes to the chest and the scars from a 'living partial autopsy' performed before she was brought to us, she is otherwise unmarred. Lisa was held in a NAD holding tank for three weeks before the interview. The subject showed markedly more or less interest depending on the gender of the attendants. As you will see in the transcript, this was the first real evidence we had of "biological needs crosswiring," as we called it in the lab. We began the interview with "How are you?")

It's funny you should say that. No one ever thinks to ask a dead person how they are doing. It isn't that zombies don't have feelings. It really isn't. Because they do.

Like, there was this other zombie chick, I didn't know her name but I called her Susan because she sort of dressed like Madonna did back in the 80's... I know I wasn't born yet, but my mom loved that movie and we used to watch it all the time when I was a kid. Anyway, I've always been good at reading people, sort of an empath, you know? Really. And this Susan, she was always sad. She didn't cry or whimper or anything, I'm not sure she had vocal cords any more, or eyes. But she had sympathetic sockets, and her facial expression never changed, but I could totally tell. She was really, really sad. So I hung out with her for awhile, especially in the beginning.

Dr. M: "Talk about that."

Well, I met Susan out near Passion Puddle, that's this pond on campus. She was standing up to her waist in the water, sort of staring out at nothing when I walked by. I always liked that pond. The legend was if you held hands with a boy and walked around it once, you liked each other; twice, you were dedicated steady dating; three times and you were going to get engaged.

I think I might have walked around it a few times by myself that morning, I'm not really sure. But anyway, a few minutes later I noticed she was following me, and we were an instant team. I'd always been the type to have people follow me around – junior high for sure, and high school on the drill team, and then in the dorm. I'd planned on pledging somewhere, but never got around to it. Heh, don't think they'd take me now. Oh, unless they have zombie sororities. Do you think they do? I mean, sisterhood for eternity, all that sort of stuff? Seems like it would be an easy match. Well, except for you wouldn't be able to sing legacy songs by candlelight, and I don't think zombies date, or drink.

Anyway, so Susan following me felt natural. But it also made me feel like I needed to lead us somewhere, somewhere she'd appreciate.

Then I recall hearing a loud constant sound, like drilling or a jackhammer or something, and for some reason it made my mouth water, so Susan and I headed that direction. I don't know why, but that steady monotonous tone really spurred me on. I think I started calling out as I got closer, too. I shouted out, "Party! Party! Follow me to the Party! Who-hoo!" That's what it sounded like in my mind. I suspect to everyone else it sounded like, you know, "Uuuuuuuuuuuuugh," or something like that.

It didn't take too long before we'd stumbled upon a group of guys repairing a patch of the road. The machines were so loud they didn't even notice us coming out of the woodline.

(Resident Eve Notes: Here the decoder noted something we now believe is similar to giggling.)

I know a girl of my class is supposed to be above this, but I've always had a thing for construction workers. Their lean, muscled bodies scintillating with sweat--as I tear into their lower abdomen to chew on a slightly alcoholic liver. Oh, how I love those rough men!

It was a perfect day. I mean, you never forget your first time, right? I stuck with just the one guy, of course, but Susan, she was… less discriminatory, is the best way to put it. I think by the time it was over she'd sampled at least a little of all of the rest of them.

Of course, after something that magical always comes the day after, and all the consequences. That's just the way it is, I suppose. You have a great moment, something you really want to remember and ride the high on for as long as you can, and then there's the accompanying reminder that maybe you didn't think it all the way through.

So, I shouldn't have been surprised to look back and find that he was following me, too. All those construction workers were, I think. Don't get me wrong, I liked having my own little posse. But Susan was one thing; a team of working boys, well, I could have done without that.

We headed north, I guess, I'm not sure why, except that the turnpike was familiar and plenty of easy pickin's there. After a month and a half, or two months, maybe three, I lost count, I finally ditched most of those guys in the Hudson just north of the upper Bay. We were a bigger group by then. Come to think of it, I think I might have lost Susan there, too. The current must have caught her. I sank to the bottom and just walked across, but she floated a little bit. I bet she ended up on a tropical island somewhere. Stuff like that never happens to me.

Anyway, back to the construction guy. I was so glad to finally be rid of him. I don't know how many hints I had to throw at him before he finally caught on. There are only so many ways to moan, but I like to think my tone was obvious. Besides, he wasn't my type.

The truth is, he wasn't something you'd stick with. No, my thing has always been for guys in uniform, and that didn't happen until later. By the time I lost Susan, I was hanging with a fairly large party. When we finally met up with the NYC bunch though, wow, that was intense. It was like a giant undead-palooza. Sometimes you could just lift your feet up and get carried along with the crowd.

We lost a few as soon as we left the city. Well, maybe more than a few. I guess they had some sort of ambush set up or something to pick us off. We weren't even doing anything at the time. The whole thing was very confusing, and loud, especially loud. Not the sort of loud you hear so much as feel. I spent most of the time bouncing around, not sure where to go, at least until the smoke cleared.

I remember there was this one soldier from New York I met in this little suburb north of the city. There were a lot of soldiers there, but this one really caught my eye. He kept shooting everyone else in the head – a real sharp shooter – but he took one look at me and just shot me in the chest.

It was so sweet... His face was wonderful.

Dr. M: "Describe it."

A little salty, peppered with dirt to give it texture, and a hint of French coffee from earlier that morning. It was exquisite. His ear, though, it had a bitter aftertaste and was all hairy... gross. I moved on after that.

A girl's gotta have her standards.

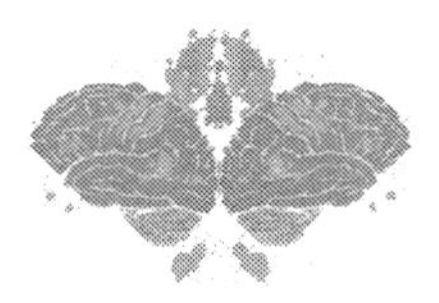

Day 24

Case Study "Sam McGee" and "Janis"

Interview #1

(Resident Eve Notes: Subject "SAM MCGEE " is a 33-year-old deceased male of Jewish European decent in NAD Stage 2. He has short thick dark hair and dark eyes, with several superficial cuts across his face. His business partner and common-law wife, "JANIS," is a 38-year-old white female, also in NAD Stage 2, with long brown hair and burn scars over 20% of her remaining flesh. In addition, she is missing her entire left arm, severed at the shoulder. Both names are their stage names, which they insisted on using. This was our first attempt to attach two subjects to each other through the decoders. Given their close personal relationship, we thought connecting Sam McGee and Janis together would facilitate the communications. There was no need to prompt Sam McGee, he began transmitting as soon as we turned on the scanner.)

Sam: Been a while since anyone wanted to interview us.

Dr. M: "You're both still interesting people."

Janis: Ex-people.

Sam: The sad thing is, we made our living mocking the undead. It was easy money.

Janis: It really was.

Sam: You know, I'd pull one sleeve down further than the other, put on a wacky gimp, scrunch up my face and say something like, "I sure had a hard day of shambling about dark buildings, looking for places to hide from the sun. So, after dark I decided to go out and have myself a Black Russian. Smooth and sweet, but hard to find. I settled for a Bloody Mary...."

That's funny stuff right? The crowds ate it up.

Heh heh, saying "crowd" and "ate" in the same sentence never felt so… Hey, you wouldn't want to lean down here so I could whisper this to you, would you?

Janis: He's not going to do it, dear.

Sam: Of course not. That would have been too easy. Do I even have a stomach any more? Eh, I can't tell. I don't think I do.

I'm babbling, aren't I?

Janis: Yes, yes you are.

Dr. M: "So tell me, what attracted you both to specifically zombie humor?"

Janis: To Sam's original point, we live in terrifying times. Horrifying times. I mean, ZOMBIES?!? That used to be hard to toss out in casual conversation. And people need to be able to smile or whoever survives is just going to crash as a society. I'm just sayin', when you run across a teenager, freckle-faced kid not even out of high -school, who ran out of ammo by noon and spent the rest of the day fending off a horde with a lead pipe, or worse yet defending himself with the leg of his Uncle Henry, well, that guy needs a laugh.

Sam: And a drink.

Janis: A drink and a laugh. That's where we came in.

Sam: And now, a public service announcement from the Surgeon General of the United States:

(Resident Eve Notes: Sam mentally made his tone overly-flamboyant and Janis chimed in, unable to resist the cue. We were very excited we had been able to fine tune the equipment enough for this level of detail.)

Janis: My fellow Americans, even though the number of people with NADS has declined dramatically in recent years, we must remain vigilant. Report any strange or unusual symptoms to your local death panel. Always remember to use safer death practices. Cremation: It's not just a good idea; it's the law.

Dr. M: "I remember that bit from a few years back. On the radio. It was funny."

Janis: Before Cremation actually became the law.

Dr. M: "Right."

(Resident Eve Notes: A moment of silence passed with the decoder picking up flashes of previous performances from both subjects along with an emotion the decoders recorded as depression.)

Dr. M: "Janis, you had an interest in those afflicted with Athena's Disease before comedy, correct?"

Janis: Well, I…

Sam: Don't say it.

Janis: I actually have a Masters of Arts.

Sam: Geek.

Janis: Yes, I am a geek. Anyway, my thesis was on the seemingly dichotomous relationship between the 19th century fascination with death as both horrific and beautiful, and how that contrasted with the view of zombies in modern society and modern representations in the media.

Sam: Really big geek.

Janis: Really dead geek.

Sam: Pity we weren't poets.

Janis: Dead poets? That's funny. You're a funny guy.

Sam: So I've been told.

Janis: We should do this for a living.

Sam: If we were living.

Dr. M: "So Janis, what would you write in your paper differently now if you had the chance?"

Janis: I'm not sure I'd write anything differently. The media was both partially right, and totally wrong. I mean, obviously I'm a zombie, but I'm not an idiot. Yet I would still give my soul, if I still have one, or if I ever had one, to bite off one of your kneecaps right now.

Sam: Man, that does sounds good.

Dr. M: "I notice that when you talk about food, particularly about me as food, your tone changes. Why do you think that is?"

Sam: I'm not sure.

Janis: I don't know.

Sam: I don't know. On the one hand, making people smile still feels like an important thing to pursue, and I still want to do it. But taking a big chunk out of your arm right now, that's… that's more like a serious need I can't ignore. At all.

Janis: He has needs.

(Resident Eve Notes: Again Janis' tone changed slightly, and this time Sam followed suit.)

Sam: Oh, do I have needs. You remember what they say about Maslow's Hierarchy of Zombie Needs, right?

Brains.

Brains.

Brains.

Brains.

And, Brains.

Just doesn't seem as funny as it used to. And really, I never even liked brains. More of a lungs man myself.

(Resident Eve Notes: A few moments later the system developed some sort of feedback loop between the two subjects that shut them both down for the rest of the day. Without expanding on the technical details, the glitch was an electrical one, and after replacing a fuse and making a small software adjustment, the equipment was up and running the next day.)

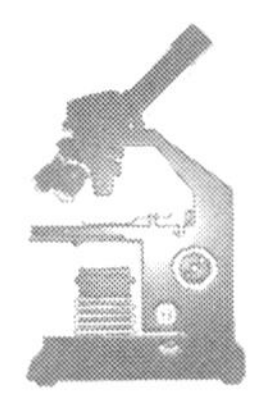

Day 26

Case Study "Sigourney"

Interview #12

(Resident Eve Notes: Subject "Sigourney" responded, over time, to more and more complex sentences. After a few weeks we were able to have near real-time colloquial conversations.)

Dr. M: "Even though you don't have a scientific background, you were considered one of the foremost authorities on NAD behavior even before your research in the field. What's changed since you've contracted the disease?"

Lots of things, really. For one, I'd published that all Reanimates craved brain matter as their primary food source.

(***Resident Eve Notes: In early interviews with Sigourney, the software incorrectly translated Reanimates into the more generic "Zombie." We discovered the distinction and made the correction at interview #7.)***

Many of the leading necrologists also thought that way. My unbelievably, incredibly non-scientific article, "Alpha Zed" described in detail how I had observed that each horde had an inherent leader.

I guess that was my bias more than anything else. There just aren't a lot of creatures in the animal kingdom that don't have a leader, unless they are primarily solitary. Reanimates move as a group, tend to want to gather together and move as a mass; ergo, they must have a leader.

I looked at movement patterns from satellites for the big picture, and from traffic cameras for urban areas. Please don't ask me how I got either of those things without a budget. Oh hell, I'm dead, who cares any more – I either stole them, promised fame and fortune for them, or I or someone on my team promised sexual favors for them. No one ever delivered on that as far as I know, by the way.

Anyway, nothing from any of those sources. So then I looked for cues that Reanimates would get from each other. We released Nosy back out into the wild – okay, again, illegally, deal with it – to see if there was any difference for a Reanimate with no olfactory perception. Nothing.

Just when I thought it was time to conclude no actual leadership role in the bigger hordes, I got another idea based on feeding patterns. In any group of more than one Reanimate, whenever they fell upon some prey – that's a nice way of saying Mr. Perkins from down the street – inevitably the same Reanimate would get the brains, and the others would divide up the rest. The one that got the brains, the "good stuff," as it were, must naturally be the leader. In the article I mentioned that this leader was gender non-specific. In fact, it was everything non-specific. A teen girl Reanimate of any ethnicity could just as likely be in charge of the group as a body builder of any other ethnicity. From that I deduced that a leadership role did exist, at least in smaller parties. If it existed there, then even if I hadn't worked out the exact details, I reasoned that it probably also existed on the macro level.

And I was totally wrong.

Dr. M: "How so?"

Different tastes. That's it. Some just like the taste of other organs better.

Dr. M: "Then why go to all the trouble for an organ so well protected?"

Hey, it's not THAT well protected, believe me.

Dr. M: "Do you prefer brains?"

Are you offering?

Dr. M: "If we could stick with the…"

Believe it or not, it's the more intelligent, or more socially responsible, Reanimate that goes for the brain.

Dr. M: "Go on."

Well think about it. If you scoop out the head, no new Reanimates running around.

Dr. M: "Safe slaughter, as it were."

Well. isn't it?

Dr. M: "So, you view this as a favor?"

More of a service, actually.

Dr. M: "How very socially responsible of you."

Thank you.

(Resident Eve Notes: The issue of differential diagnosis is a recurring problem among mental-health care professionals. Diagnosis related to undead behavior has only begun to be explored very recently, and mostly confined to the four walls of my cleanroom. At this point in the interview process, I personally was ready to diagnose Sigourney and the others with Cannibalistic Addiction, although Dr. Marshall wouldn't commit to a differential at this stage. Like most addictive behavioral disorders, Sigourney's syndrome involved

1. ***Compulsive behavior verified with obsessive thoughts brought out in therapy – the addiction dictated the entirety of their socialization and relational behavior. It ran their unlives.***
2. ***Rationalization of and justification for their behaviors – creating moral excuses for themselves as "special" and "entitled" to the activity.***
3. ***Increased frequency and depth of dependency)***

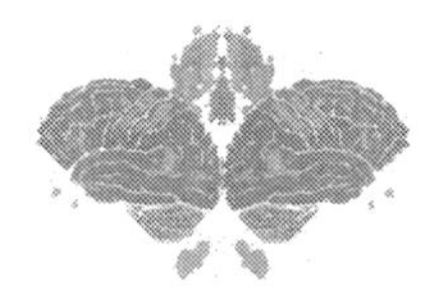

Day 27

Case Study "Dead Eddie"

Interview #1

(Resident Eve Notes: After a simple scientific curiosity bloomed into an epidemic, then pandemic, and finally to an international crisis, all the announcements still to this day call it a **crisis under control.** ***From everything I've seen, it feels more like a war to me, and probably a war we are losing.***

That's one of the things I remember best about my dad. He was one of those armchair warriors who never served in anything but professed to know everything about the military. He used to laugh when people called it a war. "Yes," he'd say, "we as a nation yielded a certain amount of territory early on, and sure a few smaller countries had to be temporarily evacuated, but I believe these were all sound, strategic decisions with an overarching plan behind them." According to his 'detailed research,' the decision not to employ nuclear weapons was based on the advice of every tactician consulted; all unanimously agreed that weapons of mass destruction were overkill. The best minds in the Pentagon worked round the clock to verify their findings.

The Pentagon fell about three weeks ago, which I include as background before we get to the next interviewee.

Subject "DEAD EDDIE" is a 41-year-old deceased white male in NAD Stage 2. He wears his jet-black hair in a regulation crew cut. His face bears severe pock-marking, presumably from some childhood illness, and his mouth and lower jaw have both been smashed with some form of large blunt object. He's lost both arms at the elbow, reportedly from a chainsaw attack, and has several gunshot wounds to his neck and shoulders. A master sergeant in the New York Army National Guard, he had served overseas during his military career, but was horribly mangled and then turned while fighting in one of the earlier local conflicts with the northeastern hordes. All communications with him failed until we referred to him by his self-given nickname. We began the interview by implanting satellite footage of the horde cutting across upstate New York.)

You're wanting to know why we "wandered" up there, aren't you? I hate it when people think we just aimlessly "wander" across the planet. "Oh, they're zombies, they just wander around eating whoever they come across. They're stupid zombies. So easy a zombie could do it." Ignorant living fascists.

(Resident Eve Notes: Emotions the computer decodes as aimless rage and frustration pass by for nearly twelve minutes. We prompt, "So you didn't wander?")

No. We had a plan. You don't have to believe me, but we had a plan. You don't win forty-two campaigns in a row without a plan. The strategy was brilliant.

Dr. M: "Go on."

Old Gray Eyes, as I like to think of him, he was a natural leader. I'd have followed him anywhere. I think he was a lawyer before he turned too, not even military. I never followed a guy in a suit before.

Now his Executive Officer, Half-Head Harry, there was something wrong with that guy. Don't get me wrong, his brain was all there, and the lack of face and an ear didn't bother me, but he had behavioral issues. He had been a soldier… my platoon leader, in fact, before some sorority girl latched on to his face at Yonkers about ten minutes before I got my leg bit.

By the way, biting in the leg, that's genius. You don't stumble across tactics like that by accident. Laying on the ground, pretending to be a corpse until some hapless idiot ignores you and gets too close. No, you have to teach someone that level of ruthless combat efficiency. That's exactly what I'm talking about.

But Old Gray, he knew tactics. He knew war. You could tell it in the way he moaned. Once he looked back, the core of his whole campaign became crystal clear. It's like Buddha said: "When they eat, attack. When they sleep, attack. When they run, really really attack." I think. Or maybe that was Sun Sue. I'm not sure.

You could see it in everything we did. First, we'd move all day and all night. None of this rest and cool off your feet stuff the way the U.S. Army does it, no way. And everyone, every man, woman, child, they were soldiers, real soldiers. Everyone walked the same distance, the same route, and if someone got left behind, well, they caught up later. Although, secretly I think some of those "left-behinds" were part of Old Gray's plans.

See, usually we just overran the targets. Little sleeping suburb with a few sandbags and mid-life-crisis guys with shotguns, that was just too easy. But sometimes they'd seen us coming, and they were ready, really ready. They'd have pits dug and filled with spikes – "Oh no! Not spikes!" – or brick walls covered in razor wire, or watch towers. Watch towers were tough ones, I admit. But also the most comedic. I mean, we weren't goin' anywhere, so it was just a matter of time before someone at the top realized they weren't getting rescued or more shipments of canned beans anytime soon. When they understood that was the end, they either jumped down for the Crowd Surf from Hell, or capped themselves and just dropped. Either way worked for me.

But in the situations where they had all that stuff, all combined together, and plenty of ammo, whenever the fighting got rough, and I thought I was going to end right then and there, that's when it would happen. Old Gray would have seen it coming, known where the enemy would be, known their weak spot, and sent a squad, or a company, or hell sometimes just one guy or gal to sneak up on them at just the right moment. I don't know how he did it, but he did it every time.

They would be firing up the countryside, just tearing us up, using some of the biggest loudest collections of war machines since The Big One, taking us out ten or twenty at a time, and then surprise! One of us biting their commander from behind. Oh, the look on their face! Priceless, really, like we were cheating or something.

U-S-A! U-S-A! U-S-A!

Yeah. Classic.

But you didn't just see Old Gray's genius in the battles. You saw it between the battles, too. Like once, when we crossed this muddy field, all 15 million of us, after we got the other side, Old Gray turned us all back around and we went through it again, walking side by side, knee deep in the stuff. Then we did it again, and then again. I lost count around thirty the number of times we crossed that same field. Obviously a ploy to conceal our numbers and our direction of movement. See what I'm sayin'?

That's when Half-Head went berserk. I think that one little patch of brain that showed through his hair had been out in the breeze a little too long. He started biting this tree. I mean like, really savagely attacking it. I admit, the way the limbs swayed back and forth did look delicious, but they were scrawny limbs without any sort of meat on 'em. That's a problem.

Old Gray and the rest of us moved on after that. Far as I know Half-Head is still there, still trying to eat that tree.

(Resident Eve Notes: After a few moments of silence, we injected the image of a tank firing into the darkness.)

Tanks, heh, those were the least of our problems. It was the bigger guns...

(Resident Eve Notes: Dead Eddie struggled to find the right word and eventually gave up. The computer retrieved several large orange clouds flying up near his vantage point, most likely from some type of army artillery shells.)

I mean, those noises and bright lights, they were so frustrating. It made sense that food would be near them, right? But no. Not once. You'd see a bang or two, wander out towards it, and then they'd be exploding all over the place. Boom, ka-pow, ka-something else-ooey. I wouldn't have minded if they'd had someone nearby to tide us over until they got all that stuff out of their system.

And those explosions stupefy the brain; you feel as if you entrails were being torn out, your heart twisted and wrenched; the shock seems to dismember your whole body.... Actually all those things really happened.

But even though you got me, I know Old Gray Eyes is still out there, plotting, planning. He's got something cooked up for you, for your families, for this whole country. Man, you just wait.

(Resident Eve Notes: Dead Eddie was the first case we had where NAD behavior manifested itself as not only something that needed to be justified, but as something that needed to be embraced and proliferated. Dead Eddie clearly had no problem transitioning from one of "us" to one of "them," and quickly taking up The Cause. I first noted it as an exceptional case, owing Ricky's similar behavior to a long practice of repeating corporate rhetoric as a coping mechanism. We would soon learn how off that initial impression proved to be.)

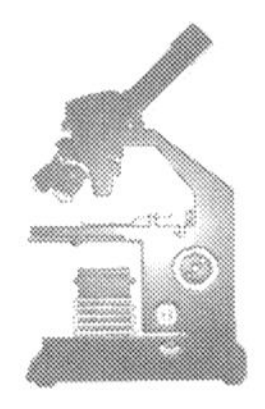

Day 33

Case Study "Ricky"

Interview #3

(Resident Eve Notes: While Ricky's face remained utterly stoic, the computer decoded what appeared to be a spike of what could best be described as happiness once we turned the scanners on. It should be noted that while all subjects retain their lungs and diaphragm, and therefore an approximation of breathing that allows an ability to draw air in and out of their nostrils, very few subjects retain what is widely accepted as the "keen zombie sense of smell." Ricky seemed to be one of the few to show advanced olfactory abilities.)

Hey, Doctor M, how's it goin'?

Dr. M: "Fine, thank you for asking. And you?"

Given I'm dead and strapped to a table, everything's great. Least I'm not a head in a jar.

Dr. M: "Valid point. What would you like to talk about today?"

Actually I'm glad you asked that. There is something on my mind I've been going over all day.

Dr. M: "Go ahead."

I'd like to talk about you, Clyde.

Dr. M: "If you wish."

Yeah, let's talk about you. I want to know what drives you to spend day after day, hour after hour, listening to the ramblings of corpses who were such losers in life they couldn't even figure out how to avoid a bunch of dead people shuffling on about as fast as… fast as… well here, let me put it this way:

One day a zombie stumbles into a zoo. Most of the animals run away, except for this one giant tortoise. The zombie falls on top of him and since he can't bite through the shell, just lets the tortoise carry him along. Know what the zombie says?

Dr. M: "I give up. Tell me."

"Wheeeeeeeee!!!"

Yeah, that's how slow zombies are. And these idiots you're interviewing couldn't find a way to get out of the way of that.

I know, I know, you're looking at me asking yourself, how am I any different? Why aren't I like these other sheeple?

Dr. M: "I wasn't thinking that, but if you'd like to explain I'd be willing to listen."

Whatever. The answer is, two reasons. First, some walking corpse didn't catch me, I was tricked by another living, breathing human being. Second, I'm not sure I mind so much.

Dr. M: "Interesting."

In fact I know I don't. I don't think MOST zombies mind so much.

And I think you're secretly jealous, to tell you the truth. All your worries gone in a single instant. Credit card bills, publish or perish pressures, grant money, all gone… You don't even need a place to sleep, 'cause you don't sleep. And yet, you still get to walk around in the fresh air and enjoy it all. Every day. Every single day, Clyde. And you wouldn't believe how much patience I've developed in just a few months.

"Oh, what about my research? My findings?" Yeah, like you've done any real research. I'm dead. Now there is an official piece of paper somewhere that says, "He's dead."

My GOD! That's brilliant!

Dare I say genius?!?

No, but certainly above average.

Every time you come in here you smell the same way, Clyde. Like you eat the same thing for lunch, Caesar Salad with garlic, Caesar Salad with cheese, today you kicked it up a notch and went for a

Chicken Caesar Salad. Hmmm, yummy. And I haven't smelled a woman on you once, if you know what I mean. You're single. You smell old, too. Old and single. Old, single and listening to dead people. Wish I could have signed up for that life plan when I was a kid. Sweet.

Dr. M: "This hostility you are directing towards me. What do you think is causing it?"

Nothing's causing it, I'm a hostile guy. That's who I am, that's what I do. Although, hostile takeovers, so to speak, are a lot faster now. And taste better.

But we were talking about you. You didn't answer my question.

Dr. M: "Ricky, let's not make this about me. I'd like to know why you are so interested."

C'mon, help me out here. What drives you to do this? Seriously. I mean, do you REALLY think you're going to help anyone in this situation? Really?

Dr. M: "I believe that the work I'm doing will some day…"

Oh, I can't believe you caved so quickly. What a crappy psychiatrist you are. C'mon, I bait you, you turn the conversation back to me. I bait you again, you turn it back again.

Nope, you just up and answer the question.

Too easy, Clyde. Too easy.

Comments?

Anyone? Anyone? Hel-looo…

(Resident Eve Notes: Rather than validate, acknowledge, or encourage this behavior, Dr. Marshall took that opportunity to terminate the interview.)

Day 34

Case Study "Richelle"

(Resident Eve Notes: Subject "RICHELLE" is a 38-year-old deceased Hispanic female in NAD Stage 2. Her dark hair is cut at about the chin level, and she is what most would consider quite attractive if not for the significant tear from the left corner of her mouth up to her ear she received during a sniper attack. She was not bitten, but rather turned after a tragic lab accident in the San Francisco NAD Research Center. We began the interview with, "Tell us about yourself.")

I remember the transformation quite vividly. I took just shy of a lethal amount of caffeine right at the end so I would stay awake and remember it all.

My one last contribution to science.

I shouldn't have bothered. One tiny little cut and suddenly two master's degrees and a PhD became the experiment instead of watching it.

The ultimate of ironies. I mean, I was one of the first in the field! Long before the San Francisco Center I was way ahead of the curve. Most of the more obscure symptoms – discoloration of the extremities, erections lasting for more than four hours, alien hand syndrome, anal leakage, loss of appetite for non-meat foods, gas with oily spotting – that was me. I catalogued those. No one else had put it together.

But maybe I deserved to get turned.

If I'd published my findings sooner, if I'd had a few more test subjects... But back then everyone denied it existed. "Isolated incidents in remote corners of the world." If the news had gotten out and Athena had heard about the symptoms, maybe she would have realized that her thirteenth internationally adopted kid wasn't just incontinent and moody. Remember that one public lawsuit with the nurser-for-hire and the breast feeding incident? That wasn't milk that kid was after…

So really, that was my fault. I don't even normally watch the Academy Awards, but something compelled me to that night. As soon as she walked out on stage I knew what was going to happen. That walk, that stare, the make-up that showed even through one of those filters that blurs everything. And they all ignored it, probably thinking she was on the verge of a nervous breakdown or weak from dieting too much.

There were even rumors they were HOPING something would go wrong, to add some scandal to the show, boost the ratings, double the income from reruns. Well they got it all right. She stood at the podium, then came slow slurred speech, faint, thud, pretend to try to cut to commercial – that last part, they must have rehearsed it just in case, you know, to add to the drama – and then she rolled over into the orchestra pit. She didn't FALL into the pit, she rolled into it, on purpose. When the screams started, I think especially when that comedian got sprayed head to toe with the blood of first chair flute player, then they really did cut to a commercial. Everyone had seen enough by then.

A few days later, when it was about to really get out of control, the media demanded to know how something like this could have happened. Every night I went to sleep terrified some reporter would call and ask if I'd known – if I had known and not said anything.

For weeks I dreamt of Athena's voice, screaming at me over the din of a bunch of invisible kids in the background. Then, in the dream, I'd wake up and the kids were all around my bed, with designer PJs and bloody teeth. Once it was bloody PJs and designer teeth, but that hardly matters.

Flash forward a couple of years and I'm standing there looking at a pool of blood in my hand and a cut in my surgical glove covered in a dryer, darker brand of blood. Shards of that stupid glass container all around my feet and the top of the table.

I felt like I could feel the virus running through my veins. Slowly, the itching spread all up my arm. For an instant I thought of trying to cut it off. Like, jamming another piece of that glass up ahead of the path of the vein before it delivered those little buggers to my heart. All psychosomatic.

Dr. M: "Obviously a very traumatic moment for you."

Yeah. I guess.

Dr. M: "What happened after that?"

I agreed to the testing, of course. Part of my penance for being so careless. Signed all the paperwork, let them shackle me to the bed, let them cover me in electrodes and sensors and everything else.

They fed me whatever I asked for, no matter how gross it was, and put wet washcloths on my forehead and played soothing music in the background. Tommy Kilmore – a lab techie I was totally crushing on – even read me stories when I couldn't sleep at night.

Then I was talking to him, and my words got slower, and slower, and then I felt numb, and calm, like I was in a dream. I didn't even notice I had his fingers in my mouth. He'd fallen out of my line of sight, I guess.

God, somebody must have been fired when I made it outside. Again, probably Tommy's doing.

But always the scientist, I set about to learn what I could do to help the NAD community. That's the sort of thing I like to do. I study, and my observations help people.

Dr. M: "Really? Any success on the front so far?"

Absolutely, although nothing completely concrete… Anyway, I observed that the biggest affliction zombies seemed to face was what I termed SEHS, which stands for Sudden Exploding Head Syndrome. There were very few symptoms that I could catalogue other than the abrupt and spectacular one at the end.

I admit I have trouble concentrating now, and whenever I saw a case of SEHS, it was not uncommon to be in a situation with a lot of noise. It was very frustrating. I'd be there, and someone's head would burst, but I'd miss it because some yummy loud crack would have distracted me for a moment just prior.

Always the same. Bang, pop. Bang, pop. Noise, head explodes. Noise, head explodes. How was I supposed to discover anything in a situation like that?

And one day, I think the day you all caught me, actually, I thought I was really on to something. There was this one sign I discovered--

(Resident Eve Notes: A fuzzy image comes into focus of a sign hanging outside a junior high that reads, "Warning - the zombie outbreak is caused by a virus spread through human contact.")

-- I knew was important, but I couldn't quite figure out what it was. I studied it, every crevice of it, in complete, silent contemplation. Perhaps there was a clue there, hidden, possibly in the lettering, something about how this virus moves from one person to another....

I never cracked the code though.

(Resident Eve Notes: Richelle, having lost at least some of her cognitive abilities, and particularly the ability to read, continued to strive for the normalcy of her life through ongoing, if completely futile, scientific research. I empathized with Richelle, wondering what I, too, would do in that situation. Hopefully it will never come to that, or if it does hopefully, Zach or Dr. Marshall knows how to wield a fire axe, one or the other.)

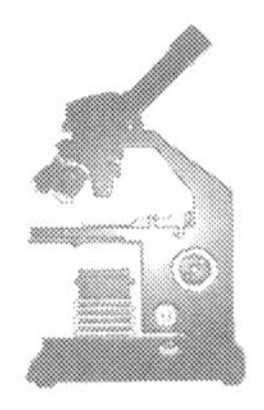

Day 42

Case Study "Sigourney"

Interview #26

(Resident Eve Notes: Subject "Sigourney" required more and more time to recover between sessions. By interview #20 she had passed into NAD Stage 3, the stage most commonly associated with bouts of actual rage. She demonstrated that, with effort and practice, the violent mood swings could be at least partially controlled. However, given the readings we have on her now, at this point we estimated only another month or two before she passed into NAD Stage 4.)

Dr. M: "Do you need anything?"

No, thank you.

Dr. M: "Are you sure?"

YOU MEAN OTHER THAN TAKING A BIG CHUNK OUT OF…

(Resident Eve Notes: No images accompany the two minutes and fifty seven seconds that followed this outburst, only waves of color – red gradually changing into purple.)

Sorry. Yes, I'm okay.

Dr. M: "Last we spoke, you were talking about when your feelings towards Reanimates, as you refer to them, had changed. I was wondering if we could talk a bit about that. Is that okay?"

I don't know where to start…

Dr. M: "Why don't you start with the Center in San Francisco."

Okay. By then I'd stayed with the northeastern horde on three different occasions. The first two for a week each, and the last one for nearly three. Before that we'd flown overhead in a company helicopter and shot a GPS transmitter we got off Ebay into a few of the larger males and tracked them so I could always meet up again with the same group.

Usually I looked for one I called Gadget. I called him that because he'd been stabbed with a couple of screwdrivers that still protruded from his sternum. I figured he was into tools and creating stuff with his hands. Regardless, both his legs worked and he could keep up with the horde, but he moved slower than most. His one eye always seemed so thoughtful.

People with Athena's Disease, and it is a disease, were always treated so harshly in the media and movies and books. I figured if I could show people how they really acted, record their behavior, that might change things.

On that third trip in, though, we ran into a group of bounty hunters. Sycophants.

Dr. M: "Can you expand on that?"

I understood their argument. In theory, the need to regulate the environment, that argument, but they were enjoying it. They even brought beer.

I didn't say anything until the stories hit the press. I did a six -part series which by episode number two boosted our advertising revenue to three times the norm. They gave me a 10% raise and covered my expenses. That's it. As I predicted, they tried to do follow ups with the younger, perkier set of reporters. When they asked me to coach them through how to blend in, I quit and wrote my own memoir of the event. Which, as you know, *Undead Like Me*, was number one on the New York Times Bestseller List for eight weeks and got translated into every language you've ever heard of, including Apache.

But while I was still writing the memoir, living off my savings account, I couldn't get those bounty hunters out of my mind. So I complained to the local police, and they laughed at me. I complained to the Mayor, and she laughed at me. Then I complained to my state representative and senators, and they fell down, rolled over and then laughed at me. I took it up to a group of lobbyists for hire and they didn't laugh. They quoted me a fee so high I figured I could build a research lab if I had that sort of cash lying around.

Then it hit me. That was what I needed to do. From that moment on, we were dedicated to making the San Francisco NAD Research Center a reality.

I still didn't have the advance on the book yet, so I had to gather all my old buddies on the weekends. We tried hiding photographers in the woods at first, but we lost two in as many days and abandoned that idea quickly. Instead we set up remote controlled cameras, and took shots of me in the horde. Me standing there among them, safe, you know, away from the sensational blood frenzies that always made the news.

Dr. M: "What about the controversy over those photographs?"

They weren't doctored. Well, I mean, we moved Gadget's arm up a little to make it look like a sort of half hug, but the rest was real.

Dr. M: "What about the allegations that because of your unique methods and situation that you were misleading the public into a false sense of security?"

WHAT ABOUT YOUR BIG OL' ADAM'S APPLE IN MY TEETH?!?

(Resident Eve Notes: Four minutes of colors pass by, orange and jagged at first, finally flowing into sheets of slow-moving blues. It was unclear if this soothing color technique was an actual technique, or a visual representation of something more basic.)

I had to do something. And when they got Gadget with a chain gun and joked about making a pot-holder or a lamp out of his head, well, that was it.

That image of me safe in another zombie's arms… I used the money that picture generated to start the Gadget Foundation to support anti-zombie-hunting laws. None were ever passed unless you count the misdemeanor charge for explosive tipped arrows. Small victory there.

But by then the Zactivists had latched onto the idea.

Day 43

Case Study "Jonathan"

(Resident Eve Notes: Subject "JONATHAN" is a 27-year-old deceased Chinese male in NAD Stage 2. Jonathan's hair is cropped short on the sides but fairly long on top, and he still bears the crisscross burns from an electrified chain link fence across his face. This interview was actually conducted by one of the less-experienced graduate students without professorial supervision. While that individual was subsequently fired by Dr. Marshall, we've decided to include the transcript regardless. He began the interview with, "Describe zombie life, as it were.")

I do NOT use the "Z word" when I talk about them. There are plenty of other terms to choose from: Breathing challenged, Reanimate, I think even Undead American would work. I prefer Reanimate.

I don't think people really understand them, and it isn't fair. When you think about it, they are a pretty advanced species. There is no racism, sexism, or religious intolerance among Reanimates. They are inherent environmentalists, with a zero carbon footprint. I don't think a lot of people understand that either. I think most Zactivists just want to get messages like that out to the world.

We're working on six different class-action suits on behalf of Reanimate rights right now. Plus we have two civil rights lawsuits pending against people who killed Reanimates based on their own personal bias. We know we'll never be able to stop the hunting of Reanimates entirely, at least not in my lifetime, but the act of hunting them shouldn't be fun. It shouldn't be a sport. It shouldn't be a way to work out daily job frustrations. That's just wrong.

The real travesties, though, are the corporations. It didn't take very long for them to figure out Reanimates made the ultimate source of free labor. You probably didn't know that, did you? Yeah, you wouldn't think treadmills linked to generators would generate much electricity with a zombie on it, but if you put 100,000 of them out there, with just one living person sitting on a chair reading a book in front of them, they keep going and going and going, twenty-four seven.

We spent weeks trying to sneak into one of their "energy-reclamation centers" to get some footage of one of these places. They ignored us and ignored us, and when we finally got our one shot, they took us in and gave us a tour of the ground floor. Plenty of cubicles, plenty of manufacturing space, but no sign of where the energy was coming from. I snuck off from the group, though, just for a few seconds, and I'm telling you I could hear moaning, deep sorrowful moaning, coming from one of the air vents. Probably a whole underground complex nobody even knows about. Probably not on the building plans, either.

They gave us hats with the New Biotech logo on it, plus some cheap-ass pens, also with their logo, and ushered us towards the door. Then the next night on the news – on a TV station that they own, incidentally – they claim they've found a way to reduce their energy intake. And no one questions how they are doing it? Despicable.

Then there's the product testing, the military weapons targeting, plus the whole crash-test dummy market – actually legal in Michigan and Wisconsin, by the way. There are even rumors that they deliberately *create* more Reanimates when the captured ones break apart. I only know one way to create new Reanimates, and I'm fairly certain no union would put up with that.

No, they have to go down, and in a very public trial.

There's precedent to support us, too. In *Snyder v. Romero*, the state of California ruled that since Reanimates had once been people, that their basic human rights – life, liberty, and the pursuit of happiness – were not inherently voided by the onset of Stage 2 Necrotizing Ambulation Disorder.

Grad Student: "Life?"

Such as it was, sure. Although that ruling was overturned at the Federal level, it set some pretty important groundwork.

When we started the League of Reanimate Enlightenment, or LORE, we were able to raise enough money to create the San Francisco Center in under two years. Think about that. Just two years. People who had friends or loved ones turned, no one wants to watch Aunt May or Grandpa Jones used as targeting practice. We rallied their support and became a force to be reckoned with in Washington.

And no matter what you hear on the news, those "500,000 strong" Breathing Normative anti-LORE rallies they all talked about, there were fewer than 10,000 people there. Every time. They were sensational, and made good headlines, but there just weren't that many of them.

And I wish I could find whoever coined the term, "Zed-hugger." That slur campaign really did some damage, especially when the press discovered Undead Heads and for their own sensational needs, they linked them to us. We're still trying to recover from that one.

Still, I'm not going to give up the fight. In a few more years, I think I might move up to lobbyist and get in where it really makes a difference.

Grad Student: "You do realize that you are a zombie?"

Very funny.

Grad Student: "No, really."

Sure, use their affliction as a joke.

Grad Student: "Your entire lower torso is open. And empty."

Stop it!

Grad Student: "If I lean down enough I might echo."

Stop it! STOP! IT! I'M NOT A ZOM … I'm not one of…

Grad Student: "I'm sorry, I thought you knew."

This is getting less and less funny.

Grad Student: "I think you're going to need to come to grips with your condition."

Now you're just being life-ist.

(Resident Eve Notes: As misguided as the grad student's efforts, I think this interview revealed some interesting traits. Jonathan showed the most complete denial of any of the subjects. I suspect this was a representation of suppressed bias against the very groups he sought to support in order to relieve his own guilt at despising them.)

Day 45

Case Study "Ricky"

Interview #6

(Resident Eve Notes: Ricky's attorneys gave us notice that they had a court order granting them access to "New Biotech property," and that they were coming by this afternoon to observe one of the sessions. Apparently, corporations like that can afford to hire minions to sift through scientific journals for information that might be related to them. That's how they stumbled across some of the preliminary reports of our research. Since the court order was not specific on how many attorneys could be in the room, Dr. Marshall pointed out the delicate nature of the equipment and how extra people would tax the clean room fans and filters unnecessarily. They agreed that only one attorney, Augustus [name redacted], would need to be physically in the lab during the session. The same court order gave him the right to review, and to some extent edit, my notes for publication. Such edits are included in brackets.)

Dr. M: "Okay, the system is up and running, and we are recording. He can hear you, and you can see his responses on this screen here."

(Resident Eve Notes: Under Dr. Marshall's guidance, we deactivated the voice simulation and provided the attorney access to text responses only.)

Augustus: "Gentlemen, I'm Augustus [name redacted] the third, of the law firm [17 names redacted], PLLC, attorneys for the Estate of Richard [name redacted], a Deceased Person. Hello, Rick."

Ricky: Hey, Gus. How's it hanging?

Augustus: "Let's set a few ground rules. First, my client will not be testifying under oath. The reliability of this equipment has not been verified, for one. Second, he is incompetent to give sworn testimony due to his status of being currently deceased. No offense."

Ricky: None taken. Some of my best friends are dead.

Augustus: "Moreover, nothing my client says should be construed as an admission of criminal or civil liability regarding any persons he may or may not have eaten."

Dr. M: "I thought he was property. Is he a client now?"

Augustus: "At this moment I represent his estate, which includes him, therefore making him my client."

Ricky: Can someone dangle a limb in front of my mouth while you two are discussing this incredibly important point?

Augustus: "Ricky, if you don't mind…"

Ricky: Ugh. Eat a lawyer. Never mind. There are some things even a zombie won't do.

Dr. M: "Is there any particular line of questions you'd like me to ask Ricky?"

Augustus: "No, no, I'm here only to observe a regular session."

Dr. M: "A regular session would be confidential, court order or not."

Ricky: It's okay. I've got nothing to hide.

Augustus: "He means he has nothing to hide from his counsel. Specifically, me."

Ricky: Oh yeah, we're close. Hey, do you know the difference between a soulless, brain-sucking, baby-eating zombie and a lawyer?

Augustus: "By 'baby-eating' my client meant…"

Ricky: The briefcase… Get it?

Dr. M: "Ricky, is there anything you would like to talk about today?"

Ricky: Wasn't I just talking? Is this thing on?

Dr. M: "Yes Ricky, but I think now might be a good time for you to explore old relationships. How long have you known Augustus?"

Augustus: "As Ricky's counsel I'd like to formally request no questions about his past employment, past projects, past involvements, or hypothetical relations with any of the employees of New Biotech. For their privacy, you understand."

Dr. M: "Actually, under these circumstances, I'm not sure we will be able to get anything substantial out of this interview."

Ricky: You guys are killin' me. Someone toss me a kidney while you waste my time.

Augustus: "What my client meant to say was that he respectfully disagrees with the premise of your statement."

Dr. M: "I'm terminating this session."

(Resident Eve Notes: The scanner remained hooked up to Ricky, and Augustus requested a few moments alone with his 'client.' I don't suppose it is any more odd for him to refer to Ricky as a client as it is for me to refer to him as a subject or patient. Even though there are a hundred ways I could have left the machine secretly recording with Augustus none the wiser, for some reason I honored their request and disabled the recording feature. Fifteen minutes later, after a number of signatures on some incomprehensible paperwork, Augustus left. We went back and continued the interview, again recording.)

Dr. M: "Are you feeling all right after all that?"

Ricky: I'm fine, Clyde. The bigger question is, why did you chase him away? I know you don't like me, and you know I want to suck your brains through a straw, so what's to hide from the legal types?

Dr. M: "I never said I didn't like you, Ricky. You are important to me. Also, I have no idea if there is anything to hide from your corporate lawyers, but my task here is to study you, and his only purpose seemed to be to hinder that study."

Ricky: Hey, did he look as nervous as he smelled? It's hard for me to rely on sight anymore.

Dr. M: "Why would he look nervous? You're securely restrained."

Ricky: You tell me. You're the shrink.

Dr. M: "Is there something he doesn't want you to tell me?"

Ricky: You tell me. You're the shrink.

Dr. M: "Clearly you are baiting me, again, to delve deeper. Why don't you just tell me what's on your mind?"

Ricky: You're not even a good shrink.

Dr. M: "I'm not here to play games, Ricky."

Ricky: You probably really turned the recorders off during that part he and I were alone together, didn't you?

Dr. M: "In fact, I did."

Ricky: Ugh. You are killin' me.

Dr. M: "I'm more curious about why you don't want to tell me something than what that something is."

Ricky: You're the one who said I had something to hide.

Dr. M: "Actually, I said you didn't want to tell me something."

Ricky: Same thing.

Dr. M: "If you say so."

(Resident Eve Notes: The interview stagnated from there and we terminated it early. Something about the readings on Ricky's comments bothered Dr. Marshall though, and he asked Ph.D. Resident Zach and me to look more into Ricky's background. Since New Biotech couldn't have anticipated the neural decoding software, they couldn't have been worried about someone pulling corporate secrets out of his mind when they ordered the bag-and-tag mission which eventually landed him here. Dr. Marshall asked Zach and me to focus on what Ricky had done since becoming a zombie, in the event there was something in his behavior that New Biotech might have wanted to stop.)

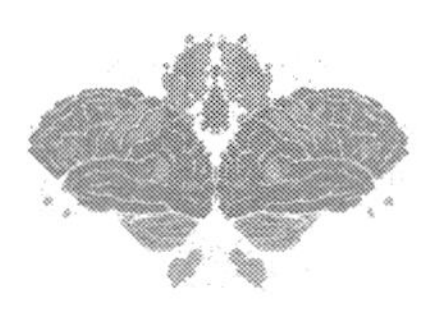

Day 46

Case Study "Marie"

(Resident Eve Notes: Subject "MARIE" is a 52-year-old deceased white female in NAD Stage 2. From the left side, Marie seems almost the grandmother next door. The right side, however, is mostly missing. The flaps of skin were surgically cut off, making her appear like some sort of very lifelike anatomy teaching aid. Her stomach region has been entirely ripped open, requiring a special brace to keep her internal organs from spilling out. We began the interview with, "You were actively against zombies in your lifetime, correct?")

The Bible, of course, and the Torah, the Koran, all the great texts, they all condemn zombies as creatures of Satan. I don't remember the exact verse, but I could give you the name of someone who could look it up for you. But everyone who has ever studied the Good Book agrees, the walking dead are evil. I guess that sort of goes without saying, but you'd be surprised how many times we were forced to say it. So much so, in fact, we started a whole support group to spread the word.

The group grew fairly quickly, I guess, but it felt like it took forever. A few knitting partners here, a PTA there, and finally whole churches. Once you got a whole church on your side, there was no stopping it. We held bake sales and garage sales to raise money, and that helped a little bit. But it still wasn't enough to do anything on our own. I think Mr. Webster first suggested that we push for a national membership.

That turned out to be a lot harder than it sounded. Some of the other groups didn't necessarily agree the walking dead were totally evil. Some thought just their actions were evil, and some thought they could be made good, and some even thought that they were evil, but we should turn the other cheek in hopes they would learn from that. Turn the other cheek, can you imagine?

Fortunately, the bulk of us, the real flock, all believed that they were evil. We did the, "This is your brain being eaten by Athena's Disease" commercial, if you remember that one. Although, we wanted the name changed to Magdalene's Disease, since Mary Magdalene was the first prostitute and all. Prostitutes are famous for spreading horrid diseases, and evil begets evil, as they say.

We also pushed that bill to try to get a zombie abstinence program mandatory in all the schools. The kids – not ours, those of others, the ones with lazy parents – they were really tempted by the whole undead mystique. I know because I studied them. You can't fight sin until you understand what you're fighting. I did a lot of interviews with teachers at our local schools, and at one point we passed out questionnaires at a table in the hallway of the high school. If you filled it out, we gave you a bag of three home-baked cookies. So now I'm up on all the lingo the kids used for their zombie-loving groups: Undead Heads, Zed Heads, Grays, Bloodies, Stiffs, Stiffies, Shamblers, Moaners, Moanas, Z-men, Zack-pack, Zackariahs. They all thought it was a righteous calling.

That's what you get when you set your baby down in front of the TV on Sunday mornings so you could sleep late instead of taking them to church. The networks programmed special zombie cartoons on Saturday and Sunday mornings, you know. We video taped several hours of it and played it back on fast forward, and you could see it plain as day. In the blur that went by, the boys' cartoons were blue or black, the girls' cartoons were pink or yellow, and in between, the commercials, gray and red. Yes, a sickly dead-looking gray and a bright blood red. Oh Honey, that really struck a note in us, I'll tell you.

And don't think it was a coincidence that last year's action figures and dolls were particularly pale, either. No, the corporate mouthpieces denied it, but we knew better.

We organized the March of Souls on Washington last year, and had nearly a million people turn out. But Congress – you know Congress – between the Zed-huggers and the fat corporate lobbyists, there was no room for God-fearing law-abiding citizens.

So we took matters into our own hands.

Most of the time we just put out fliers, spoke at schools, showed up at any of the town hall meetings, that sort of stuff. Then Ms. Bradford – she lived down the street from me and would bring over the most wonderful liver-meringue pies…

Dr. M: "Excuse me?"

What?

Dr. M: "Are you aware you just said… never mind. Interesting. Please continue."

Anyway, one day Ms. Bradford found a container of infected blood in her son's room. Some other kids at school brought a bottle as part of a science fair project – they got special permission – but once all the other kids heard how hard it was to get a sample, every-one wanted one. Anything "forbidden" was an instant attraction.

That was the last straw, and we knew it was time for stronger measures.

Ms. Bradford really wanted to show those networks what their shows were doing. None of the networks were physically near us, but one of their research labs, you know the ones that breed the infernal creatures, that one was just on the other side of town. We had the tools and we had a target. We just weren't sure how to do it.

At first we thought about holding a special bake sale in their lobby, but we figured they'd either not give us permission or it would be pretty obvious where all the contamination was coming from. And we knew better than to involve anyone else in our planning. We were willing to go down as martyrs, but it would be unfair to share that with everyone else.

Dr. M: "Another curious word choice. Go on."

Yes. Well, when Ms. Bradford's youngest daughter overheard part of the conversation, that actually turned out to be a blessing in disguise. She made the suggestion, and even volunteered to do the delivering. She had the outfit already from some work the summer before. We must have stayed up all night uncapping those water bottles and sort of gluing the caps back together so they wouldn't look tampered with.

After the outbreak on the tenth floor, well, they learned their lesson right then and there. When that hit the media, everyone blamed the Zed-huggers, which was fine by me. Everyone in that building, all the Afflicted, God love 'em, they got what was coming to them.

Evil begets evil.

Dr. M: "And how do you explain your current condition?"

This? I'm being tested, is all. The most faithful always get tested. But with my upbringing and my beliefs, I'm going to come out of this just fine.

(Resident Eve Notes: While Marie's case was interesting in its own right, our more immediate interest came with additional insight into Ricky's background. I'm ashamed to admit this breach of professional etiquette, and forced myself to take several notes on topics to follow up with Marie should Dr. Marshall take my opinion. In the meantime, the next day Ph.D. Resident Zach and I presented Dr. Marshall with more disturbing news about who was becoming our most disconcerting patient.)

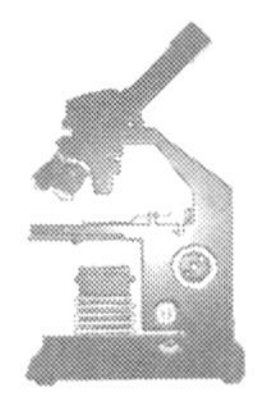

Day 47

Case Study "Ricky"

Interview #7

(Resident Eve Notes: Before continuing to Ricky's Interview #7, I thought it important to include the information we presented to Dr. Marshall. I recorded the conversation concerning our findings with an open microphone to Ricky.)

Dr M: "Eve and Zach, if you could share your research with us, please. Ricky, you may chime in at any time."

Ricky: Can't wait.

Resident E: "It was mostly Zach."

Resident Z: "Well, given the parameters you gave us, we had very little to go on at first."

***Dr. M:** "If you could explain those parameters for Ricky's sake."*

Ricky: Oh yes, do tell.

***Resident Z:** "Specifically we were told to look into Ricky's behavior since his turning."*

Ricky: Wow, get out the popcorn.

***Resident E:** "Ricky, I don't think Resident Zach appreciates that sort of commentary."*

***Dr. M:** "It's okay, Eve. Zach, please continue."*

***Resident Z:** "Well, as might be imagined, there aren't a lot of records on individual zombies out in the field. In fact, given that most tracking of the various hordes is done through military surveillance equipment, even group activity is mostly classified. Having said that, there are a number of civilian watch groups who attempt to post recent sightings to the Internet and various social networking services."*

***(Resident Eve Notes:** Ph.D. Resident Zach – normally quite the recluse – seemed nervous during this discussion, and appeared to draw strength from both his notes and the reassuring facial expressions from me. While I'm sure he understands that our relationship is a professional one – we have completely incompatible personalities – what is less clear was whether or not Zach*

was more nervous about speaking in front of Dr. Marshall or speaking in front of Ricky.)

Resident E: "Anyway, none of that mattered. None of those sites provided anything."

Resident Z: "Right. So we thought as a minimum we would start with the location where Ricky was picked up and work our way backwards. Ricky, along with several other of our current subjects, were all pulled out of the same field, where one of the larger northeastern hordes kept wandering back and forth. This activity not only triggered the New Biotech bag-and-tag operation for Ricky, but also the biggest bounty hunter slaughter to date."

Resident E: "No one ever questioned why the horde was wandering back and forth, only that their temporary circling made them easy targets."

Ricky: I seem to remember a whole hillside full of bounty hunters that got a little too cocky about the whole thing.

Dr. M: "Yes, there were scientists and amateur necrologists in that crowd, too. That part of the event made international news. Zach, go on."

Resident Z: "Well, since that was all we had to go on, we looked into everything we could there."

(Resident Eve Notes: Ph.D. Resident Zach spread a massive pile of printouts on the table and put them into several stacks. I mention this because it seemed more of a stalling technique than an actual attempt at organization.)

Resident Z: "All the people who were turned that day, none were turned by Ricky. In fact, he wasn't anywhere near that crowd that got the people on the hill. As best we can tell, the New Biotech team grabbed him and pulled him out without incident. So that was a dead-end. But then we looked at the field itself. Unremarkable in most ways, and left in its original unimproved state since before the first outbreak of the Athena Disease."

Ricky: 1,000,006 zombies walking across an unremarkable field. Sounds like a movie pitch to me.

Resident Z: "I said mostly unremarkable. We looked into the deed behind that field, and learned that it was owned by a tiny company called Junk Finders, devoted primarily to collecting scrap metal and wood and discarded household items and either somehow turning that into a profit or burying them in that field as a legal but small landfill."

Ricky: Oh, okay, 1,000,006 zombies walking across an unremarkable landfill. That's better.

Resident Z: "It was closer to 100,006, but regardless, it didn't take too much more research to learn that Junk Finders, and therefore this field, were purchased by New Biotech approximately two months after the first outbreak."

Ricky: Really? Hm.

Dr. M: "So if the zombies weren't in that field because of a co-incidence, could there have been some other reason? Some-thing attracting them there, maybe?"

Resident Z: "No way to tell from here."

Ricky: I think you might be reading a little too much into all this. Big crowd of zeds, wandering across a field, they got disoriented. Disoriented, that's all. They're zombies! I'm not sure what the question is, even.

Dr. M: "Thank you Zach. So Ricky, this raises the question, what's out in that field?"

Ricky: I'll skip the trite part where I say 'How should I know' or 'You'd never believe me,' and skip straight to telling you it doesn't matter what I say, you're going to do what you're going to do.

Dr. M: "What do you think we're going to do?"

Ricky: I'm sure I have no idea.

Dr. M: "Is there something you're afraid we're going to do?"

Ricky: I'm not *afraid* of anything.

(Resident Eve Notes: Ricky remained silent after that. A few images flashed by on the decoder screen, most related to memories of a horde shambling across the countryside. They seemed fuzzy at first, and eventually a cloud of brown closed in on the images and smothered them. It is unclear if this was a conscious attempt by Ricky, or if something else was going on in his mind, or with the equipment.)

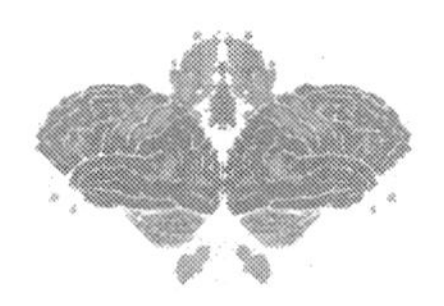

Day 49

(Resident Eve Notes: We've begun to plan a potential trip out to the Junk Finders landfill to follow up after our previous interview with Ricky. While exciting on some level, we are, as a group, not very experienced in field work. In fact, with the exception of some clinical studies Dr. Marshall did on standard human deviant psychosis about ten years ago, my undergrad expeditions may make me the veteran field researcher of the lab. I'm not sure Zach has ever gone outside beyond what it takes to get from one form of transportation to either a domicile, social activity, or a place of work.

I think Dr. Marshall may have overestimated our abilities, as he has given Zach and me the order that, given their unique qualifications and experience, we are to bring Richelle and Sigourney along with us. Making our equipment transportable was never in the original spec, so we've got a lot of work ahead of us. I personally think we're starting to push ourselves too hard, but Dr. Marshall believes that landfill holds some real significance. If we have a way to attract large crowds of zombies to a single point, we might be able to get them to move to a central location en masse, for example. He had many theories for potential applications, but rattled them off so fast that I was only able to get one of them down.

In the meantime, pressure from our underwriters for tangible results has necessitated we keep advancing our research. Dr. Marshall sat down with both Zach and me and we discussed a way to give our subjects more of a social interaction. It wasn't long before Zach came up with the obvious solution. We then shut down for another week to both make the adjustments in the equipment for that new project, and to make all the preparations for the expedition to the landfill. Again, for the record, I think we might be overworking ourselves a bit, but I believe in Dr. Marshall and his research, and I believe we're on the verge of something really big, so, I'm not complaining.)

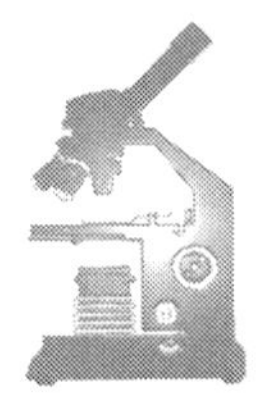

Day 53

Case Study "Group Therapy #1"

(Resident Eve Notes: After almost a week of overtime and a special group of technicians we brought in on contract, we were able to modify our primary device to decode and transmit multiple conversations back and forth. We set up a series of webcams facing each subject, and then set the software to send an image of that person's webcam to each of the other subjects. The visual aspect of seeing the face of the speaker we thought would really help the group get to know each other quickly.)

Dr. M: "Okay, since none of you, with two exceptions, have ever been hooked up together before, let's begin with some introductions. Start with your name and a little bit about yourself. Who would like to go first?"

Lisa: I will. My name is Lisa. I got turned at Rutgers after having sex with an infected frat boy.

Marie: Charming.

Dr. M: "Now now, no judgments, please, just introductions. Who's next?"

Lisa: Oh my GOD, didn't I infect you?

Marie: No, no I don't think so.

Lisa: No, I'm sure I infected you. I never forget a spleen.

Dr. M: "Who's next?"

Marie: I already started so I'll keep going. I'm Marie.

Lisa: I totally infected her.

Dr. M: "Anything you'd like to add, Marie?"

Lisa: It was during my experimental phase.

Dr. M: "Moving on…"

Janis: Does that make you a fleshbian?

Dr. M: "Ladies, PLEASE."

(Resident Eve Notes: This initial outburst I attribute to not having set ground rules up earlier. We should have treated this group like any other Group, and we failed to do so up front. Dr. Marshall attempted to remedy it right away.)

Dr. M: "OkayI can see by the way this is going that I'm going to need to emphasize a few basic tenets to these sessions. First, we're here to build trust and safety. While you can have a feeling, acting on that feeling, particularly a negative feeling, on your self or on others is unacceptable behavior. We respect each other by experiencing feelings and allowing ourselves to talk about them. Are there any questions?"

(Resident Eve Notes: A few of the monitors recorded minor indistinct emotions, but nothing concrete.)

Dr. M: "Okay, would someone else care to introduce themselves?"

Tom: I'm Tom. I was in high school.

Dr. M: "Very good. Next."

Jonathan: Hello, my name… What is that? That picture. Is that supposed to be me?

Dr. M: "Go ahead and tell us your name, please."

Jonathan: Jonathan. But that's not… What a crappy Photoshop job. Look, I appreciate what you are all trying to do but I'm not…

(Resident Eve Notes: We'd hoped that Jonathan's delusion that he wasn't a zombie would fade in the presence of other NAD sufferers, and Dr. Marshall told me to make a note to look into more intensive therapy methods in the future.)

Dr. M: "We'll come back to that. Let's continue, please."

Sigourney: My name is Sigourney, I used to disguise myself as walking dead and do stories on Reanimates.

Janis: Oh, right! I read your book. It was the last thing I ever read, actually. Nice work.

Sigourney: Thanks. I'd just like to add that I'm really glad to get to meet all of you. I mean, where I can talk to you. You don't know how long I just wanted to be able to talk to one of you. Ask you even the most basic question…

(Resident Eve Notes: Sigourney's readout swirled with emotions that the software decoded as some form of crying.)

Sigourney: Anyway. Crappy way to do it, but good to finally get to do it.

***Dr. M:* "Thank you for sharing that Sigourney. I know that was hard for you."**

***(Resident Eve Notes:* I noted, at the time, that having access to a machine that could occasionally pick up emotions felt a great deal like psychological 'cheating.' Dr. Marshall mentioned that, too, and for a short time we considered disabling any part of the decoding process besides just words. Eventually we resolved to leave the emotion readers on, because it was important to compensate for the lack of non-verbal cues a living patient would normally give off.)**

Janis: I'm Janis, by the way. I'm a… was a… comedian. Clearly.

Sam: I'm Sam, her partner in crime.

***Dr. M:* "Thank you both. Sam and Janis were the first two people we were able to hook together in simultaneous conversation, so I wanted to thank them for helping us get to this point."**

Janis: Rock on.

***Dr. M:* "Okay, next?"**

Richelle: I'm Dr. Richelle Rosenrosen, from the San Francisco Research Center. I used to study, people like us.

***Dr. M:* "Thank you, Richelle."**

Ricky: My name is Ricky, and…

Dead Eddie: Holy crap! It's Old Gray Eyes! Who would have thought this whole time I was in the same room as greatness? This guy's military genius is legendary! Man, that's awesome. I'd shake your hand… or salute… but, you know…

Dr. M: "That will do, Dead Eddie."

(Resident Eve Notes: Dr. Marshall pointed out that he wasn't surprised to hear Dead Eddie name the first dominant male personality he encountered as his fictional Old Gray Eyes. He told us that he decided to wait and explore that another day.)

Dead Eddie: Right, that's my name, Dead Eddie, I'm a soldier. But wow, awesome.

Dr. M: "Okay, very good. What I'd like to do now…"

Ricky: Let the healing begin?

Dr. M: "I think we're a long way from any healing, Ricky. Let's just start with any issues or thoughts anyone has about their current condition. Jonathan, you sounded like you wanted to go first."

Jonathan: Well I'm not sure I have anything to talk about. I mean, I've always stood up for Reanimate rights, from the very beginning. I think all of you have made some valid lifestyle choices, however repugnant to modern society, and I'm okay with that. Honestly, I don't understand why I'm here.

Dr. M: "Anyone care to reply to Jonathan?"

Sigourney: He makes me want to cry.

Lisa: Awwwwww. Me, too, now.

Dead Eddie: Makes me wish I had arms so I could reach over and slap him.

Dr. M: "Sigourney, could you expand on that thought?"

Sigourney: All that time moving with Reanimates, being near them, I never knew what they were feeling. I never imagined that inside could be a person in complete denial.

Jonathan: Oh God, you're in on it, too! Or you're just buying this ridiculously morbid picture that keeps coming up when I talk. Does someone think this is funny?

Janis: Here, let me help. Jonathan, let's pretend you're at a nice restaurant wherever in the world there is still a nice restaurant. Possibly Alaska. Anyway, the waitress is a tall brunette who is a little bit on the chunky side. She tells you the specials for the day are a massive six-meat-and-cheese chef salad, French onion soup, or the rare rib-eye steak. Which would you rather eat?

Jonathan: Describe the waitress again?

Janis: Exactly.

Lisa: Ooooh, good one!

Jonathan: That doesn't mean anything. I was just curious, okay?

Sam: Die-curious?

Lisa: Oh, another good one!

Janis: I liked Fleshbian better.

Dr. M: "Okay, let's stay focused. Anyone else have anything about Jonathan's condition that they think might help?"

Ricky: I have a question for you, Jonathan. I want to know why you DON'T want to be a zombie?

Jonathan: Reanimate, and I never said I didn't want to be one. There's nothing wrong with…

Ricky: Right. So you do want to be one?

Jonathan: Again, valid and respected life form, just like any other…

Ricky: Do you or do you not want to be one?

Jonathan: What I want is irrelevant. The point is that society needs to stop discriminating against Reanimates, however they come into being.

Ricky: Let's just play a little game of word association. I'm going to say a word, and you tell me the first word that comes to your mind, okay?

Jonathan: Sure, but…

Ricky: Dog.

Jonathan: Sigh. Okay, uh, do it again.

Ricky: Dog.

Jonathan: Uh, dead.

Ricky: House.

Jonathan: Burning .

Ricky: Brains.

Jonathan: Gross.

Ricky: Hm, intestines.

Jonathan: Hungry.

Ricky: Next case, please.

Jonathan: What? I like tripe. That's no big…

Ricky: Jonathan. Seriously. You're immortal now. Bullets can rip through your body and it won't matter. People can light you on fire and you won't feel a thing. I could throw you over my shoulder and carry you across the floor of the ocean and we'd come out the other side completely unscathed.

Sam: In about a decade.

Ricky: Jonathan, this isn't a curse. This is a gift. Rules no longer apply to you. ANY rules. Embrace it. Do you really want to go on pretending you're something you're not?

Jonathan: I'm not pretending. I'm…

Ricky: Okay, fine. You're an idiot.

Janis: That doesn't sound like healing.

Ricky: And when I say idiot, I mean you are the least common denominator of human society. Getting turned into a brainless ghoul was a step up for you…

Jonathan: Okay, now you've crossed the line!

Ricky: Well here's an idea, why don't you just hop up off that table and do something about it then? Hm? You're so hot and human and all, just get up and come on over here.

Dr. M: "Okay, I think maybe we should…"

Ricky: Or just an obscene gesture, would be nice. Just hold up an arm, and flip me a big ol' bird, huh? Go ahead.

Jonathan: I… I can't.

Ricky: Coincidence? Or sinister conspiracy? You decide.

***Dr. M:** "Ricky, Jonathan, thank you both. Now let's go ahead and move on to someone else. In fact, let's all take a moment for a little mental palette cleansing, as it were. I want everyone to take a moment to relax. Think calming thoughts. "*

(Resident Eve Notes: At this point several of the decorders recorded images of what could best be described as "easy pickin'" victims. People buried under rubble, dazed people in a car wreck, people otherwise slow or infirmed, etc. It was interesting to note the universal link the subjects had between "calming thoughts" and "easy-to-eat" people.)

***Dr. M:** "Good. Good. Everyone take deep breaths. Well, metaphorical breaths anyway. Calming thoughts. Soothing thoughts. Now let's hear from someone we haven't heard from yet. Tom? Do you have anything you'd like to talk about?"*

Tom: What? No. I was daydreaming about stumbling across some of these chicks from my old English class trapped in a room with no windows.

Lisa: Typical.

***Dr. M:** "Marie, how about you?"*

Marie: There's no need.

Dead Eddie: Oh good, another one in denial! Doc, seriously, where do you FIND these people?

Sam: Well, I mean, battlefields… mostly, right?

Ricky: Not me, I was a bag and tag special.

(Resident Eve Notes: While I didn't notice it at the time, it seemed notable in retrospect that Ricky was aware he was a "bag-and-tag" case, given the chaos surrounding his capture.)

Lisa: What's a bzardagadtack mambo banana patch?

Dr. M: "I'm sorry Lisa, could you say that again?"

Lisa: Hoooorembay wheee icky icky tang.

Dr. M: "Zach, we seem to have a problem with Lisa's connection, anything we can go about that?"

Resident Z: "Stand by."

Dr. M: "Anyone else having trouble speaking or hearing me?"

Tom: Am I okay?

Janis: Can you hear me now? Can you hear me now?

Sam: Mecka fnord lecka highdoggles.

Dr. M: "It looks like Sam's is malfunctioning, too."

Resident Z: "Yeah, it's just going to get worse. We're going to have to reset the whole system."

Dr. M: "Alright, I'm going to end it for today. I just wanted to say thanks to everyone here, and to our two Residents, for making this all happen. I believe these group sessions are going to be what this institution needs to seal in funding, nail down support, and for everyone here to get the first taste of the recognition you've all worked so hard for. Once we work out a few bugs, I think we can take this public. Just think, you all here will be the first of your kind to communicate with the outside world. For the first time, people will hear the voice of the undead as something other than a mindless moaning. Congratulations to you all."

Sigourney: Thank you Doctor, I really mean that.

Dr. M: "You're welcome Sigourney."

Ricky: Suck up.

Dead Eddie: You tell 'em Gray Eyes!

Lisa: Auwickaham whatthemuh garbage?

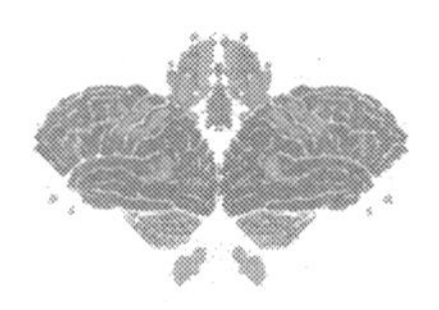

Day 54

(Resident Eve Notes: Dr. Marshall requested I write about anything that occurred related to our work regardless of whether or not it involved an interview. Actually, he and Zach either just suck at writing or hate doing it, one of the two, especially if it comes from hand-written diary notes instead of something digital. I apologize if I slip into colloquialisms, but if they want me to write, I'm going to write the way I want to. Actually, this could be good for me, as I find putting pen to paper therapeutic in a way, particularly when allowed to include my own personal introspection.

To sum up, it's a week after our last interview with Ricky. As of yesterday we've shut down in order to let some other techies do a complete overhaul on the equipment. The goal is to accommodate all the extra power and relays and computer memory we require to continue the Group Therapy sessions without any additional interruptions or technical glitches. In the meantime, for our field trip to the Junk Finders landfill, we've gotten permission to wander the countryside as part of zombie research, although we were very vague about the location in our application other than to mention tracking the paths of the northeastern hordes over the last year. From all sources we could gather, the bulk of the hordes have moved south either

into the Appalachians or down the coast. Unfortunately, on a morbid side note, according to what news we can gather, they are facing little resistance on the way.

I'm starting this journal on the three-hour plane flight to the Air Force intermittent strip west of The Desolation perimeter. Since the forecast in that area is down to less than 1 zombie per mile, and since that is about as low as I've heard in years, I feel less nervous than several of the expeditions I went on as an undergrad. I'll attempt to put the events into more prose form rather than some of the drier texts I've written at Dr. Marshall's request. I've been cautioned not to get carried away, and that "at the first word of dawn being rosy fingered," I'm fired.)

We got the healthier of the two Institute planes, although the better of anything powered by a double set of propellers hardly seemed reassuring. At least a single prop would have ensured death on impact in case of a crash landing.

Dr. Marshall hired two bodyguards to escort us, although he didn't use the Institute-approved contractor list because he said he could get a better deal elsewhere. The male of the duo was large, in both height and girth, although I couldn't tell how much of that was muscle and how much was just mass. The female was in much better shape, but with harsh angular features and her hair cropped short. They both wore vests with extra pockets stuffed full of what I hoped was ammo, and they both carried dark soft cases that obviously held their primary sidearms. Neither gave their names.

Against my protests, Dr. Marshall ordered that we not mention to either bodyguard that two of the three reinforced "scientific equipment" boxes contained the bodies of Dr. Richelle Rosenrosen and Sigourney, both in a special field expedient version of our lab set up.

"Ah, good, there they are." Dr. Marshall spotted the pair of "profiteers," as he called them, in the two Hummers waiting down on the strip.

"I get shotgun," Zach said in his customary dry tone.

"You'll be commanding the second vehicle," Dr. Marshall replied without acknowledging the joke. "You'll have one bodyguard and the scientific equipment, and I'll take Eve."

The ride wasn't too bad. The Hummers were hybrids, and we kept them on electric silent mode for the bulk of the trip. Not that they would pass unnoticed if we moved upwind of any branches of the horde, but with quieter engines at least we wouldn't pull Reanimates from every nook and cranny along the drive.

The countryside looked remarkably less desolate than the overrun cities, probably because the walking dead showed no interest in plant life or intentionally setting fires in their wake. In fact, entire crops still thrived in some of the fields we passed along the way, although now struggling against all the natural predators and competition humans had removed for thousands of years. Fields like that almost always went untended until degrading completely back to wildflowers and grasses. It was too hard to clear tall vegetation with any degree of certainty, and even with the armored harvesting machines, it only took one mistake to chop up a body and contaminate the entire crop.

"On the left." Male Bodyguard mentioned stuff like that every time he spotted a zombie. Standing in the turret, he tracked anything moving with the rifle he'd propped on the shield, but never fired. When I asked him about it, he explained that shooting usually attracted more, and headshots from moving vehicles were rarely successful. I personally hadn't fired a gun since the mandatory weapons familiarization classes in school, and wondered what it might be like to stand up in a vehicle aiming some massive machine gun on the shifting horizon. Had I still been an undergrad, I'm certain I would have asked him for the opportunity right then and there.

"Driver, see that section of torn fence up ahead?" Dr. Marshall pointed to a large barrier of metal and wood with only a few sections and warning signs still in tact. "Head through there."

The driver nodded and didn't hesitate to cross over into obviously private land. In this part of the country, property ownership meant as much as it had in 1944 Europe, but with fewer civilians wandering the countryside. Fewer living civilians.

A few minutes later and we'd stopped on a hill overlooking a pasture dotted with spires of rusted metal jutting out of the ground. Some grass had grown back in spots, but for the most part it looked like a field where 100,000 undead had trampled back and forth for weeks.

"Okay, now what?" Zach put his hands on his hips while the two bodyguards got out and took up positions out in front and behind us.

"Well, according to the GPS," Dr. Marshall checked the readings, "this is the hill of the, uh, significant unpleasantness, while the bulk of the horde gathered down there."

The two Hummers followed slowly behind while we walked down into the muddy clearing. True to what one would expect in a landfill, bits of trash and discarded appliances poked out of the dirt most of the way down. As we walked, I kept an eye out for sharp shards of metal that might cut boots or my pants leg, for fear they'd be contaminated.

"Zach, is the remote set up?" Dr. Marshall didn't turn as he spoke.

"Yep, we should be able to talk to Sigourney, uh, you know, *back at the lab*, from here." Neither bodyguard seemed to notice Zach's obvious lie about Sigourney's location.

I'd helped Zach modify the decoder for field use. Sigourney's crate contained the standard number of probes and a small transmitter that sent information back and forth to a headset on

Zach's head that fed from a mini laptop hanging by a strap around his neck.

"Good, can she see what we're seeing?"

"Negative. I have to take pictures and send them in."

Dr. Marshall seemed annoyed by Zach's reply. I guess he'd expected us to work a live video feed into her head, even though we hadn't even figured out how to manage that sort of bandwidth back in the lab. Zach went ahead and snapped a quick shot of the field and wired it through. He paused and waited for her response.

"She says she doesn't get it. There's nothing in this area that should attract a Reanimate." Zach listened a few more seconds. "No lights, no houses, no heat sources, no caves, no movement. Unless you can find something like that, she's baffled." Then Zach laughed.

"What's funny?" Dr. Marshall asked.

"She says it is good to be out in the field again, so to speak. And she doesn't even have to worry about dousing herself in old blood this time."

"Well, good," I said, at a loss on how else to reply.

"Anyway," Zach said, his smile a little sad. "She wanted to tell us thanks. Both for trusting her and for letting her be a part of something like this."

"Yes, except that she's baffled, which does us little good," Dr. Marshall replied.

"Of course, she's basing her statement on one picture." I said, a little annoyed that Dr. Marshall would cut down her efforts so quickly. "There might be other factors she can't sense through that feed."

"Right. A loud or rhythmic sound, possibly a scent, for example, Dr. Marshall added.

"Shh, you smell that?" Zach didn't actually smell anything, but I was the only one who got the joke.

We scoured for awhile down in the mud and the eight-month-old footprints. We found mostly trash. Scraps of clothing here, rusted metal shapes long separated from their original machines, a handful of bones from discarded limbs. Or so I thought.

"You know, they carried away a lot of topsoil," Zach said, staring down at the ground.

"Your point?" Dr. Marshall seemed frustrated.

"What if that was their goal?" Zach squatted and studied the dirt closer.

"First, they can't have goals. You should know that," Dr. Marshall replied. "Their minds can, but their bodies are on autopilot."

"Okay, but someone or something made them walk back and forth and back and forth here, and the only thing that did was move a lot of dirt." Zach picked up a stray metal stick and poked it in the earth.

"Dead Eddie did mention Old Gray Eyes leading them around," I said, and then quickly covered it. "A ridiculous delusion, of course, but interesting nonetheless."

"Yes, I doubt there even is an Old Gray Eyes," Dr. Marshall said, looking around. "Probably just the nearest male figure to him at the time, or a completely imaginary figure his mind created to fill a psychological need for leadership."

" But," I continued, "he might have been mentally converting some other sort of stimulus into his fictitious hero. A sound, a scent, who knows."

"Again though, whatever the cause, they moved a lot of dirt." Zach poked the dirt even deeper.

"Like if they were digging," I said, not quite meaning to speak out loud.

"Yes." Zach flipped a massive dirt clod out of the ground. "Digging for something like this."

"Do I dare ask?" Dr. Marshall voice remained aloof, but his eyes opened wide in Zach's direction.

"It's a head," Zach said. Dr. Marshall and I moved in for a closer look.

"Hundreds, maybe thousands of zombies died here once the bounty hunters caught wind of it, and then hundreds of humans after that one tiny miscalculation." I could tell by Dr. Marshall's face I should have kept that thought to myself.

"No," he said without looking up. "None of those would have been buried even a few inches down, and this one is mostly decomposed. It's probably a year old."

Zach took a picture and sent it off before speaking. "That was to Richelle."

It didn't take long before he got a reply. "She says at least two years old, possibly three, by the looks of it."

"It still has skin on it," I added. Forensics was never my specialty.

"Right." Zach tilted his head, listening to the headset. "Remember the Athena virus repels most other bacteria and insects, slows the rate of decay considerably."

"See if there are any more." Dr. Marshall took the head from Zach.

We looked around and had no problem finding bones. Most were limbs, and most rested on top of the ground, some still with clothing on them. Dr. Marshall told us those were probably left over from the most recent battle, and to pick a spot and dig, possibly in the center of the mud. It didn't take us long to find several decapitated bodies and their heads, old but still fleshy, about two feet down. Before the horde marched over the area, these corpses might have been three or four feet underground.

"Zach, get the field unit. Eve, dig through what you've found and identify the most intact specimen you can find."

"And keep your hands away from their mouths." Zach stated the obvious, but I appreciated the gesture. Even several years dead didn't always really mean dead.

He made a quick trip back to the Hummer and brought back the spare unit. We would be lucky if the hook-ups with Sigourney and Richelle lasted thirty minutes with all the dirt and the jarring around. The actual field unit we'd rated at five minutes tops. Zach quickly jammed the probes into the three-year-old head.

BLAM!

The shot startled everyone. I personally fell to the ground with my hands over my head, like that would help me in any way.

"Hey boss," Female Bodyguard's voice was unexpectedly more feminine than the rest of her. She hollered down from the smaller of the two hills. "Downwind, small group heading this way." I'd worked with these sorts of mercenaries before. They usually used "small group" to mean well over a hundred undead.

"Very good, thank you." Dr. Marshall focused on Zach. Zach took a moment before he turned back to his equipment.

"We've got a reading," he said. "A strong one too."

"How strong?"

"I think, wow, I think I could talk to him." Zach looked up, surprised. "Crap, except this unit doesn't have a microphone. All I can do is listen."

BLAM! BLAM! Female Bodyguard held her aim after she fired and didn't turn back for a second report, which was never a good sign.

"Can it record?" Dr. Marshall waved his hand impatiently.

"Yeah, yeah." Zach typed quickly as he spoke.

"Worse news." Male Bodyguard stood on the opposite hill and faced an entirely different direction. That realization made my heart skip. If there were more coming from that way too… "We got fast movers inbound."

"Can't you military types ever speak in plain English?" Dr. Marshall kept his eyes on Zach's screen.

"Helicopters," Male Bodyguard shouted down. "Two of 'em. Plain enough for ya?"

"Keep recording." Dr. Marshall spoke in a quiet voice, but loud enough I could hear. "Everyone move towards the Hummers and get ready for a quick exit."

We hadn't taken but a couple of steps before the two dark shapes came into view overhead. One up high, one close enough we could feel the wind from its rotor wash. The roar of the close one drowned out everything on the ground.

"Attention!" A speaker from the near helicopter yelled. "You are on private property!" Looking closer, I noticed the stylized green Bio-hazard symbol that New Biotech used in their logo. "You will put down anything you have picked up and vacate the premises immediately!"

BRAAAAAACK!!!!

As if to emphasize their point, the higher helicopter ripped off a ten-second burst from a chain-gun I hadn't noticed before in the direction of the "small group" of zombies headed our way. That sort of ammunition sold for almost a hundred dollars a bullet these days, and I'd probably just watched a month's paycheck fly down past that hill.

Our group continued towards the Hummers, Zach struggling to keep the head out of sight and also maintain the appropriate contacts with the probes.

"We're not entirely dim!" The voice-of-God speaker system was really getting on my nerves. "The optics up here can see your acne from a kilometer away. In the dark. Please put down that skull before you move any closer to your vehicles."

Zach only glanced at Dr. Marshall a moment before unhooking the field unit and letting the head fall back into the mud with a sickly wet thud. I glanced down and thought for a moment that I saw the jaw making slow opening and closing motions near Zach's ankle.

We loaded the Hummers without incident and both helicopters escorted us back to the edge of Junk Finders territory, where they hovered and watched us until we couldn't see them anymore, or at least that long, maybe longer.

With Zach in the other vehicle on the way back, we could only communicate via the two radios in the Hummers. He verified that all his readings from the head were good, and that he'd backed them up, and would work to get whatever information he could while we drove. That turned out to be, shall we say, overly optimistic, as Zach ended up doing little more than the initial backups. He claimed he'd attempted to get the information to both Sigourney and Richelle, but both their links cut off within ten minutes of leaving the field.

No one spoke other than those sparse radio communications and occasional zombie sightings. I had no idea what we'd stumbled upon, or nearly stumbled upon, but while Dr. Marshall scribbled notes every few minutes, I spent my time staring out the back window, scanning the sky for any sign of those two helicopters.

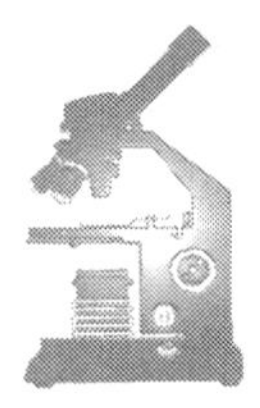

Day 56

(Resident Eve Notes: We're still analyzing the information we got from the head in the New Biotech fields. That will be Zach's realm, hopefully with whatever help we can get from Dr. Richelle Rosenrosen. Since Zach is leading that investigation, it will probably take a lot longer than I have the patience for. I'm not sure I understand all the implications of a three-year-old brain with readings strong enough to give us a signal, but it certainly had Dr. Marshall and Zach theorizing on the flight home. Once we got back on the plane, I spent most of the trip checking on the equipment linked to Sigourney and Richelle, so I missed the bulk of their initial ideas.

Dr. Marshall did commend me when I brought up a point about Sigourney's reaction to being a part of something again, however small her part in it was. We've decided the more we can use her, perhaps as a Group Therapy leader, the better it might be for everyone.

However, after the trip to the landfill, I am both emotionally and physically exhausted. I'll be taking the rest of today and some of tomorrow off so I'm rested and ready for our second Group Therapy Session. I may have to make a stern recommendation to Dr. Marshall in order to get him out of the lab

and not spend eighteen straight hours a day in his office. Meanwhile, I pretty sure Zach already crashed.)

Day 58

Case Study "Group Therapy #2"

(Resident Eve Notes: We ran the new equipment through several more diagnostic tests than normal before hooking up the subjects this time. I believe the additions will make this possible for our current group, and potentially groups as big as twice this big in the future. We attached Ricky first, and Dr. Marshall gave him a firm warning not to be disruptive to the group or we'd cut his connection.)

Dr. M: "All right, hope everyone can hear me. You all know the ground rules this time, so hopefully we'll be able to make a little more progress this go 'round than last time. Any questions before we begin? No? So, who wants to go first?"

Lisa: Well I started last time, so someone else has to go first.

Sam: That's what she said.

Janis: Ouch. Honey, is it even legal to do "that's what she said" jokes any more?

Sam: Just trying to start the meeting with… Okay, shutting up.

Dr. M: "Fair enough, Lisa. So who would like to start?"

Richelle: Do we know how long this is going to take?

Dr. M: "Let's not worry about time constraints right now, please."

Richelle: Well, it's just I'm working with Zach on a special project and it's really important and I'd really like to get back to it. I mean, I'm not sick or anything.

Ricky: Oh, no, not at all.

Dr. M: "Ricky."

Richelle: I'm a zombie, sure, but I don't have any *mental* disorders.

Dead Eddie: Cough, eatspeople, cough.

Ricky: Why don't you tell us about your top secret special project then?

(Resident Eve Notes: Dr. Marshall gave me the signal to cut off Ricky's communication for a few seconds as a warning. I blinked his feed off for an instant before reestablishing contact.)

Dr. M: "Why don't we shift to something someone wants to talk about. Does anyone here have something they would like to share with the group?"

Dead Eddie: I want to know if Jonathan still thinks he's alive.

(Resident Eve Notes: Jonathan didn't reply at first, so Dr. Marshall prompted him.)

Dr. M: "Jonathan, would you care to respond?"

Jonathan: Do we have to do this all again?

Ricky: Not saying anything this time.

Lisa: Hey! Maybe we need an intervention! I'm good at them! I had to go through like four different types with my family, so I'm totally the expert.

Marie: Four? Different types?

Lisa: Yeah, but the sexual addiction one was way out of line.

Marie: Really?

Lisa: WHAT IS YOUR DEAL WITH ME?!?

Marie: I don't have anything against you personally.

(Resident Eve Notes: The equipment spiked over Marie here, indicating a high probability that her last statement contained at least one significant lie. Dr. Marshall pointed at the readings silently and made sure we all saw it.)

Dr. M: "Marie, I think Lisa may be trying to say she's feeling singled out by you, and that you tend to respond negatively to her comments. Is that right, Lisa?"

Lisa: Totally.

Marie: I'm sorry, dear. I'll try to keep my comments to myself next time.

Dr. M: "Marie, if there's something you want to share with Lisa that is constructive, or that is affecting your relationship with her, this is the place to bring it out."

Marie: There's nothing. I mean… there's nothing.

Ricky: Oh, somebody please call her on that one so I don't get in trouble.

Marie: Well, I do take my faith very seriously, and I just don't get the impression anyone else here does.

Tom: I used to work at a bookstore and got fired because I kept stocking the Bibles under Science Fiction. Does that count?

Ricky: Who are you again?

Tom: Tom. I was in high school.

Ricky: Riveting epitaph.

Dr. M: "Marie, it is understandable to feel frustrated in a situation where you perceive others are different from you, particularly when that difference relates to a core belief or value. Is there something about Lisa in particular that makes you more angry at her than at any of the others in regard to your religion?"

Marie: No. Well, it's just that… Not really.

Dead Eddie: Out with it!

Ricky: Oh, thank you, thank you.

Marie: Okay. Okay. She just, well, she cheated me out of something very important, that's all.

Lisa: So I DID bite, you didn't I? I told you. I know my spleens.

Marie: You did bite me, sweetie. Well, you mangled my whole lower torso to be frank about it. I just didn't say anything because I was already infected.

Lisa: Would it help if I smiled sheepishly and said, "My B"?

Marie: No, no it would not.

Lisa: So I cheated you out of a long and happy life or something like that?

Marie: No. No. You cheated me out of crossing over peacefully. The way it was intended.

(Resident Eve Notes: The equipment continued to show internal conflict with Marie with every sentence.)

Marie: But the faithful get tested, that's just the way it works. Like I said, I had been infected a week already by then.

Lisa: If it makes you feel better I think I remember you being really yummy.

Sigourney: Marie, do you want to talk about your initial infection? Before you… met, Lisa. I know I'd like to hear about it if you don't mind.

Marie: Oh my goodness, no. No.

Sigourney: Are you sure?

Ricky: Not a good sign when you have to hide things from your shrink.

Marie: I just don't think this group will understand, is all.

Dr. M: "Marie, this is a safe place. Everyone here needs to understand that. No one is going to make you do anything."

Marie: I know. Just so many people get the wrong impression with my church as it is and…

Dead Eddie: You got infected in church?

Marie: I guess you could…

Dead Eddie: In a church?!?

Dr. M: "Dead Eddie, don't interrupt. Let's let her speak."

Marie: Well, a while back, right around the Second Outbreak, we got this new pastor, Pastor Jim, and he had a lot of good ideas. Really good ones. He understood how God could let something like this happen. Other people were running around screaming and wailing saying they'd been forsaken. Not Pastor Jim, he heard the Word and he *understood.* God didn't just let this happen, God *made* it happen, and not for some mysterious reason at all. No, it's very clear. It was as clear then as it is now, and after old Bob Frazier died, God love 'im, well, when he turned sour right in the middle of Saturday night sermon, that was the ultimate sign from above.

(Resident Eve Notes: Marie stopped there, and the audio ran silent for almost a minute. Almost every member of the group showed heightened agitation states, but all resisted speaking.)

Dr. M: "Marie, did you want to elaborate on that?"

Marie: Well, that night Pastor Jim said we were being called for something new. Called, I say. I emphasize that, very important. Called upon, and in order to do that, he said we needed a new type of communion...

Janis: This can't end well.

Sam: Body of Bob. Blood of Bob.

(Resident Eve Notes: Ricky, Dead Eddie, Tom, and Lisa all cried out in various levels and expressions of disgust at this point, and Dr. Marshall cued me to mute their feeds so Marie wouldn't be overwhelmed. She probably heard them start, but I cut them off fairly quickly.)

Dr. M: "Sam, Janis, everyone, please."

(Resident Eve Notes: Marie's anxiety level shot up, as one would expect, but then she became calm far too quickly for any sort of healthy coping mechanism.)

Marie: Zombies are a lot closer to Godliness than people think.

Dr. M: "In what way, Marie?"

Marie: I mean, all those nights with my husband rubbing up against me in bed, asking me to do all those… those unspeakable things.

(Resident Eve Notes: Various sexual images flashed by on Marie's screen then, although the rest of the group couldn't see them. In all cases the emotions associated with the images seemed mixed.)

Marie: Not anymore, I tell you. When you become a zombie, you give up all the pleasures of the flesh. A lot of times because you have no flesh, but your soul stays sweet and pure, untainted with worldly issues or desires. Really, why else would God have put zombies here in the first place? There is no other answer.

Dr. M: "Thank you Marie. I know that was hard for you to talk about…."

(Resident Eve Notes: At this point, I mistakenly thought it okay to unmute the feeds of the others, and did so.)

Sigourney: Yes, thank you for sharing that, Marie.

Dead Eddie: If I still had a stomach I think I'd hurl.

Sam: Right there with you, buddy.

Lisa: Gross.

Dr. M: "Everyone! Everyone, please. So, I'm going to digress for a moment, but to be clear, am I to understand that as a group, well, how to put this…. We've discussed eating spleens, livers, brains, and I believe the intestines of living humans, and each time that elicited neutral to positive responses. However, the idea of consuming even the smallest bite of skin from another zombie…"

Tom: Bleeeech!

Dead Eddie: Stop it!

Lisa: Ewwww!

Janis: Eck.

Dr. M: "But if I were to offer up the eyeballs out of my head…."

Tom: Is he serious?

Sam: That would be sweet.

Lisa: Tease! Tease!

Sigourney: YUMMY YUMMY IN MY TUMMY!! Oh God, sorry.

Dr. M: "Curious…"

Richelle: Just what do you think we are, Doctor?

Ricky: He thinks we're cannibals.

Dr. M: "Ricky, you sound like you have more to say on that topic."

Ricky: I'm just saying, you think of us as the same species, eating our own. I think we can all agree that's just not true any more.

Sigourney: Wow, I never thought about it that way. I think you might be right.

Dr. M: "How so, Sigourney?"

Sigourney: Well, we can recognize each other as different, plus we can't interbreed with living humans and vice versa.

Lisa: Speak for yourself.

Marie: Oh now, that's gross, dear.

Sigourney: Not interbreeding in the traditional sense, anyway. Isn't that how you define a species?

Richelle: I suppose we reproduce asexually – again, which is obviously different from living humans. We'd really need to get into the DNA-sequences and morphology to be certain. Wait? What did I just say?

Dr. M: "That's a very interesting theory for the group, and one I think we should dig deeper into on a later date. But for now, let's move away from the scientific topics and focus more on what's going on with you as individuals."

Sigourney: I'm learning so much. If only… if only I could have spoken with you all sooner…

Dr. M: "Don't stop there, Sigourney."

Sigourney: It… it just would have saved… well, a lot of stuff. Time.

Ricky: Hey Clyde, is it okay to change topics for a sec?

Dr. M: "I'm not sure Sigourney has said all she had to say, Ricky."

Sigourney: No no, that was it.

Dr. M: "Are you sure?"

Sigourney: Absolutely. That was my whole thought.

(Resident Eve Notes: The sensors registered quite a bit of evidence to support that Sigourney had many more thoughts on the topic, but swallowed them at the first excuse not to confront them. Dr. Marshall actually balled his fists for an instant at this lost moment with her, and made a note for us to go back to that discussion with her as soon as we could.)

Ricky: I was wondering why we can't have a day room.

Dr. M: "I'm not sure I understand your question, Ricky."

Ricky: Don't psych wards usually have a day room? Someplace we can go to be social if we want to be?

Dr. M: "Well, you can't really 'go' anywhere, Ricky."

Ricky: Mentally we could. At least in theory. You know, like a chat room.

Lisa: Our own little social networking site!

Sam: Facebook of the damned.

Janis: Don't be redundant, dear.

Sam: BiteOffYourFacebook?

Janis: Better.

Dr. M: "I see. Before this gets too far off topic, what you are saying is, you'd like some place, a virtual place, so when you wanted to get together and talk, you could, but it would be totally optional and you could leave any time?"

Ricky: You got it, doc.

Sigourney: I did read once that time spent in the company of others is supposed to be therapeutic.

Ricky: And time apart, that gets us brooding and separates us. That's not what you're going for, is it, Clyde?

Dr. M: "No, of course not."

Lisa: Oooo, or how about an online way to lure people in to meet us?

Sam: Z-Harmony?

Janis: Oh, oh, I got this one! Give me a sec. OK, ahem. "Me, eating toe and finger sandwiches in the rain, watching network sign-off reruns, oozing on birds in the park and snapping at strangers on the subway; you, stumbling and breaking your ankle trying to run away, vomiting at my cabbage-like scent; in the end, my lips meet your kidneys. Must have at least three out of four limbs. No freaks."

Sam: Oh, I wish I could clap.

Dr. M: "Let's calm down now. That seems like a good place to end for today then. I'll give this day room idea some serious

thought, and while I'm not promising anything, I'll see if we can make it work.

On another note, this is the second successful group therapy session we've had, and I want to congratulate all of you on this. Along those same lines, I really think we're ready to make this public. I'm going to be getting together with doctors Eve and Zach, and we're going to put together something for the medical community to observe. I can't tell you how important such a moment would be. Not only would it give you all the recognition you deserve, but it will help provide the funding required to keep this operation, and our contact with you, going. You should all be very proud of what you've accomplished here."

(Resident Eve Notes: After Dr. Marshall terminated the session, I continued to monitor the overall emotional output of the group. All, with the exception of Marie, seemed to radiate a sense of pleasant anticipation. I'm uncertain if this was more in response to the idea of a dayroom, or the idea of going public, or simply a response to the group atmosphere.)

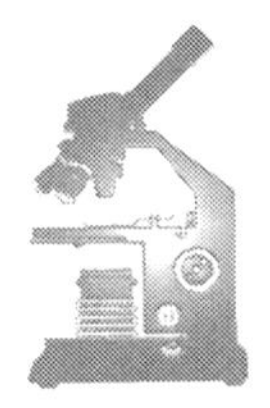

Day 59

Case Study "Sigourney"

Interview #29

(Resident Eve Notes: After the second Group Therapy session, Dr. Marshall requested that we hook up a signal light to each subject in order to let us know whenever one of the subjects had something they wanted to discuss with one of the doctors between regular interviews. I wasn't surprised when Sigourney was the first to request a session. Dr. Marshall had gone to bed for the night, so I took the interview on my own.)

Resident E: "What's on your mind tonight, Sigourney?"

A billion tiny virus cells partying and debating what horrible deed they can get me to do next.

Resident E: "Not bad. Were you waiting for that question?"

Nope, just came to me.

Resident E: "Clever."

Yay, me.

Resident E: "So that isn't why you signaled me then?"

Right, no. I was just thinking. You don't mind me sharing my thoughts do you?

Resident E: "Of course not."

Well, the group sessions have been good. I mean, they were nice and all. But like I said, it was really good to finally be able to talk to Reanimates.

Resident E: "You devoted the last years of your life to studying them, following them around; it must have been frustrating not being able to communicate."

Exactly. And well now, now that I'm finally able to do it, I'd like to do it more.

Resident E: "I assure you that we'll have more group sessions than just those two, Sigourney."

I meant more in a professional capacity. Like with you, in a session.

Resident E: "Hm, you mean as an assistant?"

Yeah.

Resident E: "Well I must say that isn't standard practice in most forms of Psychiatry."

I wrote a lot of stuff that seemed good at the time, but turned out to be total crap. I'd like my final article, my last story, to at least be accurate.

Resident E: "You could do that now. Just dictate something to Zach or me that corrects previous inaccuracies and we'll see what we can do to get it published."

Look, you know how much time I have left before I'm totally useless. I'm doing okay most of the time suppressing my Man-Eating Tourette Syndrome, but I have to concentrate almost every minute of the day, at least a little.

I admit that the virus must be doing something to suppress normal ambition and drive, because on the surface I do feel relaxed. But, when I was alive, I never actually got a chance to help one of them. Not once. People died, news outlets made money, I stumbled around covered in old blood… But I can't name one of them I actually helped. I'm not even sure there was a way I could have, or if I should have.

But now I can, in some other way than helping them go on to kill another victim. Now I can help the person, the people, because their monsters aren't around anymore.

Resident E: "You do have a significant amount of experience in the field, plus a genuine empathy for Reanimates."

Even more so now that I am one and all.

Resident E: "Dr. Marshall and I are having a session with Jonathan tomorrow afternoon. I'll ask him if he minds if you sit in. Okay?"

Jonathan… yes, the Zactivist in denial?

Resident E: "That's the one."

That would be great, Doctor. I really appreciate it.

Resident E: "Very good. I'll see you tomorrow, then."

Eve?

Resident E: "Yes, Sigourney?"

Why are you here so late?

Resident E: "I work late all the time. It's no big deal."

But Zach isn't always up this late.

Resident E: "I just like to make sure things are ready for Dr. Marshall when he gets in every morning is all."

Really? That's what you're going with?

Resident E: "What do you mean?"

Eve, I spent the best years of my life trying to read the emotions of zombies, and that was before this heightened sense of smell I have now.

Resident E: "Yeah but your eyes worked better back then and you could control where your head turned, so what's your point?"

I think you're doing this as more than just professional courtesy is all. I mean, girl to girl, you know what I mean?

Resident E: "Not exactly, no."

You like him.

Resident E: "I respect and admire him."

Oh, you've got it bad if you can't even admit it to a dead person.

Resident E: "Dr. Marshall is an attractive man, I admit, but there's nothing going on between us, got it?"

And you're good with that?

Resident E: "Yes, Sigourney. And I'd appreciate you not mentioning this in a session, just to avoid any sort of… weirdness… for lack of a clinical term."

Oh, you do have it bad.

Resident E: "I'm signing off."

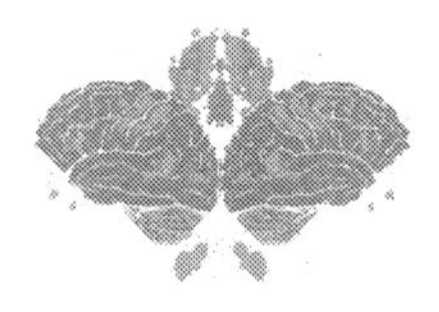

Day 60

Case Study "Dead Eddie"

Interview #3

(Resident Eve Notes: Subject "Dead Eddie" signaled that he wanted a session, and after my success with Sigourney yesterday, and with Dr. Marshall focused on other things, he let me take this one alone as well. I'd preferred to have spent the time preparing for the afternoon session scheduled with Jonathon and Sigourney, but also realized I needed to make myself available for these sorts of short notice requests.)

Hey there, Doc.

Resident E: "Hello, Eddie."

(Resident Eve Notes: As I suspected, Dead Eddie didn't respond to a shortened version of his self-given nickname. I weighed the option of turning it back on him and refusing to grant his session unless he responded to just "Eddie," but decided there was little value, therapeutic or otherwise, for that

action, other than a small sense of self-satisfaction for me if I could force him to do it.)

Resident E: "Dead Eddie, did you want to speak to me?"

Yeah. Hey.

Resident E: "Why don't you go ahead and tell me what's on your mind today?"

Well, it's just…I think something might be wrong with me.

Resident E: " You've gone through a lot of unhealthy changes. I think we can both safely say you have issues now you didn't have when you were fully alive. What specifically do you think is wrong?"

In the beginning… I mean… well, I just don't seem as excited about things as I used to, you know? For example, I really wanted us to win for a while there, and now it doesn't seem to matter as much.

Resident E: "Uh-huh."

Plus, there are other things, too. I don't feel like I have much of a future now, whereas before I really thought I was going somewhere. I guess once I learned you have Old Gray Eyes here instead of him being out leading the troops, that took a lot of the wind out of my sails. And I'm having trouble sleeping….

Resident E: "Dead Eddie, you can't actually sleep… I'm sorry, go on."

I can't concentrate like I used to, I feel really angry a lot of the time, and for a long time there, I kept seeing my hands, you know, covered in blood. Sometimes they were ripping someone apart, or doing some other unspeakable act. The same sorts of events, happening again and again.

Resident E: "You haven't had hands or arms for a number of months, and certainly not when we brought you in. However, it is probably safe to say that these aren't visions or hallucinations. You probably did rip someone apart, and you probably did have blood on your hands. You realize that, right?"

Plus I'm pale. I mean I know I'm dead, but I think I'm pale even for a zombie.

Resident E: "Dead Eddie, you just listed textbook examples of symptoms of PTSD.

I've got it, don't I? I thought I might. Oh, man, the PTSD. Personal Traumatic Stress Disease.

Resident E: "Post Traumatic Stress Disorder."

You won't tell the others, will you? Especially Old Gray?

Resident E: "No, this session is confidential, at least as far as the other subjects go. But this is nothing to feel shame about."

What can we do, Doc?

Resident E: "Well, first I must say it is encouraging that you asked. That's a good sign. Most treatment would revolve around getting you to recall the events in question, express your feelings, and gain a feeling of control over the event."

Oh, hey, I know how I can recall the event.

Resident E: "Good. We'll get to that in a second. I'd also like to add that you might gain quite a bit by bringing this up in our next Group. Studies have shown a lot of recovery happens when people with similar experiences share their thoughts and emotions."

No, I think I need to focus on recalling the event. That's where I'll get the most healing.

Resident E: "What did you have in mind?"

Can we walk through a similar-type scenario and see how it turns out?

Resident E: "We can try that. How would you like to begin?"

I'm not sure I've actually seen your picture, Doc. My eyes don't work so good any more.

Resident E: "All right, hold on a second."

(Resident Eve Notes: Without considering the consequences, I quickly scanned my ID badge picture and transmitted to Dead Eddie.)

Is this what you look like now?

Resident E: "My hair is darker now and up in a bun, but other than that, pretty much."

You're a real looker, Doc.

Resident E: "If we could move on."

Right, so maybe if you could talk me through a scenario, maybe one in my past, and I'll try to picture it. See if I can work through my emotions. Tell you what I'm feeling.

Resident E: "I'm assuming that because you asked for my picture that you'd like me to place myself in this scenario, yes?"

Oh yeah, that'd be yummy.

Resident E: "Yummy? Really?"

Just an Army slang term. That means that would be ideal.

Resident E: "So you want me to sit here and describe to you a scenario that involves you attacking me?"

Yeah, oh yeah. I think that would really help.

Resident E: "And of course, the more vivid the detail, the more it would help you?"

Absolutely, yes.

Resident E: "Of course."

(Resident Eve Notes: I admit that I might have gone along with it for a few sentences if I hadn't been able to 'cheat' and see some of what else was going on in Dead Eddie's head. I could tell his pleasure centers were over-stimulated even without the monitors to tell me so.)

Resident E: "Dead Eddie, you worked with other veterans before you got Athena's Disease, didn't you?"

Yes. How did you know that? Can you see that in my brain?

Resident E: "Just taking a wild stab in the dark on this one. Out of idle curiosity, what sort of work did you do with other veterans?"

Handed out pamphlets, mostly. Sometimes got them in to see special doctors. You know, shrinks and stuff.

Resident E: "Dead Eddie, you do realize that the symptoms you listed were exactly the sorts of symptoms one might read off a pamphlet."

Yeah, you said I had it already.

Resident E: "Eddie, I'm going to end this session now."

What? No! Why?!?

Resident E: "I believe you know why, Eddie."

No! What about the healing?!? I need some endorphins to get me through this…

(Resident Eve Notes: I admit that I started calling him Eddie on purpose, at least partially to get back at him for wasting my time for his own self-indulgence. I was beginning to feel that the subjects more readily took to me as a peer or friend than Dr. Marshall. While I'd appreciated the frankness of Sigourney, the interview with Dead Eddie made me want to take his head off his body, carry it outside and kick it around like a soccer ball.)

Resident E: "For the record, neither I nor any of the other doctors appreciate attempts at manipulation. Please keep that in mind for next time."

Couldn't you just pretend to get caught in a dark alley for a few moments?

Resident E: "Good night, Eddie."

Oh, have a heart, huh? Can't you help a guy out? Just a little…?

(Resident Eve Notes: I noted Dead Eddie's behavior in his file. I also made a point to see if someday in the future he would try anything similar with either of the two male doctors, or if this sort of thing was gender specific. Fortunately, the success we had later that afternoon took my mind off the Dead Eddie unpleasantness.)

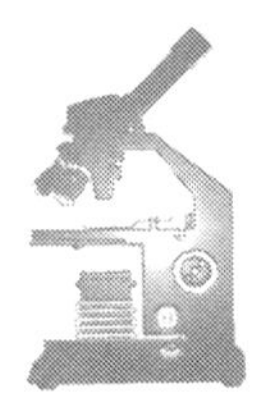

Day 64

Case Study "Sigourney and Jonathan"

(Resident Eve Notes: Sigourney actually sat in on two sessions Dr. Marshall had alone with Jonathan, both of which led to very little progress and no commentary from Sigourney beyond the cursory introductions. I suspect she was hesitant to join in either because of her newness to psychotherapy, or because she honestly couldn't think of anything to say. Another option was that she was expending all of her energies trying to suppress her desire for random violent verbal outbursts. Finally, on the third session, right after an abbreviated Rorschach test, she spoke up. In that session, Dr. Marshall had decided to go only with black and white ink blots.)

Dr. M: "Jonathan, I'd like to begin today by discussing what I believe is your obsession with human internal organs."

Jonathan: Not again.

Dr. M: "I'm going to show you an image, you tell me what you see, okay?"

Jonathan: Sure, whatever.

(Resident Eve Notes: We started with the standard blot I.)

Jonathan: Uh, am I allowed to turn it?

Dr. M: "Of course. Let me know which way you want it rotated and I'll make the adjustment."

Jonathan: Upside down.

Dr. M: "Better?"

Jonathan: Yeah. That's a pair of lungs.

Dr. M: "And this one?"

(Resident Eve Notes: Standard Ink blot V)

Jonathan: Uh, kidneys.

Dr. M: "And finally this one?"

(Resident Eve Notes: Standard Ink blot VI)

Jonathan: That's a brain, from the top looking down on it.

Dr. M: "Do you think you have an obsession with human organs?"

Jonathan: Me? You're the one who keeps showing me all the graphic pictures!

(Resident Eve Notes: Dr. Marshall paused here for a moment, presumably to regain his thoughts.)

Sigourney: Doctor?

Dr. M: "Go ahead, Sigourney."

Sigourney: Jonathan, this is Sigourney. Do you mind if I ask you a few questions?

Jonathan: Are you kidding? You were the whole reason I became a Zactivist.

Sigourney: Thank you, that's very sweet.

Jonathan: I mean, I kept a copy of your book in every room of the house, and passed it out whenever I found someone who might read it. The word had to get out, you know? People needed to understand it was all right to be a Reanimate, and they shouldn't be discriminated against.

Sigourney: Thanks.

Jonathan: So, shoot.

Sigourney: Jonathan, I'd like you to think back for a moment about the last happy memory you had.

Jonathan: The most recent one?

Sigourney: Yes. The most vivid happy memory.

Jonathan: Uh, lessee. Me and my girlfriend, Julie. We were at a party somewhere, in someone's backyard. There was a fire in the chiminea, everyone was all dressed up. I think there was jazz music in the background.

Sigourney: And do you remember whose party it was?

Jonathan: No. The details are a little fuzzy. But I think we just knew we were supposed to be there and everyone was cool with it.

Sigourney: It's sort of like a dream, isn't it? A little hazy around the edges, but all the rules are perfectly clear, right?

Jonathan: Yeah, exactly.

Sigourney: Now Jonathan, focus on the party, did you notice a lot of the color red there? Did anyone seem angry at you, even though you didn't feel like you did anything wrong?

Jonathan: There was this one couple, they must have been drunk. I remember I was talking to the woman, and the guy was screaming at me. He was a jerk.

Sigourney: What color was the woman's outfit, Jonathan?

Jonathan: Actually it was red, now that you mention it. But I think that was sort of the theme of the party.

Sigourney: And the man, what did he do?

Jonathan: He kept hitting me with something, a fire poker I think, smashing me and Julie with it like a crazy person.

Sigourney: Do you remember any pain?

Jonathan: No. I just assumed it was a plastic fire poker, or that he was just really weak.

Sigourney: Good. Now, do you remember anything you had to eat that night? Maybe something the woman in the red outfit gave you? One of your favorite foods?

Jonathan: These little red French dark chocolates filled with brandy. I love those things. And she had a whole tray full of 'em.

Sigourney: Jonathan, I want you to think further back now. Think about all the happy moments you can remember before you came to this place. Can you remember any of them that didn't involve little red French dark chocolates?

(Resident Eve Notes: Several images flashed by on Jonathan's screen, most too hazy to confirm, but many with tell-tale hints of blood and chaos.)

Jonathan: No, actually, there has been a lot of that lately.

Sigourney: Now Jonathan, this is important. Without relying on your memory of those events, do you really believe those chocolates come in the color red?

Jonathan: Well, I'm not… I mean… I can't think of any in stores...

Sigourney: And someone hitting you with a metal fire poker. They don't make them in plastic, so that should hurt, shouldn't it?

Jonathan: Yeah, that makes sense.

Sigourney: And parties don't usually have a red color theme to them do they?

Jonathan: No… no but...

Sigourney: With me it tastes like chili dogs with mustard and onions.

Jonathan: What does?

Sigourney: After I turned. After I died and woke up again. The first time I got a hold of some poor bastard jogging with head-phones on who didn't see me in the bushes. He tasted like chili dogs to me, Jonathan. It took me a week to realize he hadn't just randomly stopped to put on a red shirt and dance with me on the running track.

Jonathan: Oh, God.

Sigourney: It's all right, Jonathan. There's nothing you can do about it now.

Jonathan: It's true. It's really true. I didn't want to… I mean, there could still be some sort of mistake, right?

Sigourney: Jonathan, I went through exactly what you're going through now. We all did.

Jonathan: Oh, God. This is really horrible. I never thought I'd actually… that was just for other people. Oh, God.

(Resident Eve Notes: Jonathan's screen jolted with a series of confusing images and swirls of colors. Dr. Marshall decided that as significant as this breakthrough was, we'd gone far enough for the day and Jonathan could use some time alone to process his thoughts. I turned off Jonathan's equipment but left Sigourney's running.)

Dr. M: "Thank you, Sigourney, that was extraordinary."

Sigourney: Really? I did alright, I guess.

Dr. M: "You did more than alright. That really reached him. Although…"

Sigourney: What?

Dr. M: "Please tell me you made up the chili dog part."

Sigourney: Uuuh…

Dr. M: "Oh my, you were serious, weren't you?"

Sigourney: Actually, only men taste like chili dogs to me.

Dr. M: "I beg you not to…"

Sigourney: Women taste like cookie dough ice cream.

Dr. M: "Well, I think I've heard enough for one night."

Sigourney: You don't think there's something Freudian in the chili dog thing, do you?

Dr. M: "Thank you for your help, Sigourney. You did something really good this evening."

Sigourney: Whatever I can do.

Dr. M: "Yes, I suspect that's true. Now, if you please, good night."

(Resident Eve Notes: I feel it my duty to note how Dr. Marshall pulled me aside to mention how truly impressed he was at Sigourney's abilities that night. He reviewed the monitors and pointed out how he could tell she was battling emotional turmoil the entire time and it never showed outwardly. He mentioned that there is a real strength of character there. It makes me wonder what I'd look like – how I'd compare – if put under the same sort of scanner.)

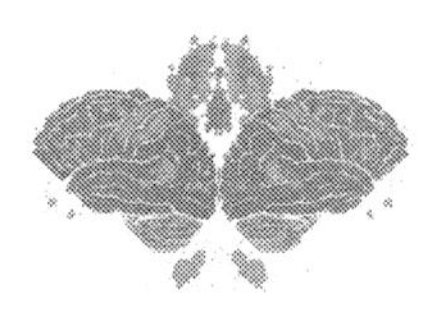

Day 66

Case Study "Ricky and Richelle"

(Resident Eve Notes: Yesterday we were served with something called a "Writ of Sequestration" by the local sheriff's office. Apparently, we have to appear in court in 14 days to show cause why we shouldn't have to turn New Biotech property (Ricky) over to them immediately. Our lawyers countered by filing a motion to dissolve the writ, arguing that a) Ricky isn't property; and b) that Ricky doesn't actually belong to New Biotech. We think this will draw it out as long as another month, maybe two. Bottom line, what this means to us is that our time with Ricky may be limited.

In response, Dr. Marshall set up a meeting between himself, Zach and me, Richelle, and Ricky. Richelle, in this case, turned out to have valuable insight in a sort of "idiot savant" fashion. New topics, written words, those all confused her tremendously, but any reference to something in the purely molecular biology realm, and it was like she was still in her lab.

Zach, Richelle and I had wanted another day before presenting our findings, but we were close enough, Dr. Marshall felt, for an update. Before we started the interviews, we down-

loaded some of the initial findings into Ricky so we could gauge his reaction.)

Dr M: "Okay, as you all know, the clock is ticking. Let's talk about what we found. Zach, if you could lead things off, please. "

Resident Z: "Right, so, up until this point, all of our experiments with zombie mental capabilities give results that graph the timeline as about one year of normal, albeit disassociated, brain activity before the cerebellum degrades enough to move the subject into the deranged NAD Stage 3. After that, another month to six months before the completely feral NAD Stage 4."

Resident E: "The readings from the head we found in the Junk Finders field combined with the tissue samples we retained on the probes now tell us something different. It seems, at least with that one subject, that NAD Stage 2 brain activity can continue at least as long as thirty months."

Ricky: I can only hope you have a Power Point presentation ready to go with all of this.

Resident Z: "Actually I did, but, um, Eve said that would be obnoxious."

Ricky: Good for you, Eve.

Resident E: "Thanks. But back to the point – faced with this anomaly, we decided to send the data from our tests to Richelle to see what she could make out of it. Richelle?"

Richelle: By way of background, the virus normally surrounds the brain, the spinal column, and motor nerve endings with an envelope of oxygen, so when the body dies, the brain tissue can continue to send impulses to the rest of the body. The virus intercepts and takes over a lot of those impulses to create the ruthless brain eaters we all know and love, but still. The virus also feeds off any flesh that enters the victim's mouth or stomach, and digests it to provide some of the other nutrients a brain needs to function, usually by physically carrying those nutrients like very slow blood.

Ricky: Are you guys going to talk equations soon?

Richelle: Gradually, the virus dies and can't keep up with the needs of the brain. The virus dies in a pattern, developed over maybe as much as 10,000 years worth of evolution. This is a lot for a virus if you think about how far the flu has come in a few hundred years. Anyway, this pattern allows the decay of the least important parts of the brain – cognitive thoughts – first, and to the virus, the most important parts of the brain – motor skills – last.

Dr. M: "Thanks, Richelle. And so what is the implication with this new subject?"

Resident Z: "Sorry to interrupt, but if I may? The implication is that this is a stronger strain of the virus. One that can live longer, or is more efficient in providing for the needs of the brain, keeping it functional much longer."

***Resident E:* "But here's the best part. We think that if this virus infected a person before they died, the extra oxygen flow from this stronger strain would mean the virus could keep the entire brain functioning."**

***Dr. M:* "So no disassociating the higher brain functions from those that control base bodily functions?"**

Richelle: Better yet, potentially not even a need for the virus to kill the subject.

***Dr. M:* "Are you suggesting a vaccine?!?"**

***Resident Z:* "Not exactly. A vaccine would put lesser strains of the virus in so the body could develop its own defenses. This would put in a stronger version of the virus that would simply keep out the previous one. According to our theories, this super version wouldn't need to shut down the body to survive. The infected person would be a carrier, still very much contagious through blood or sexual contact, but functioning normally and very much alive."**

***Resident E:* "Until they died."**

***Resident Z:* "Yes, thanks, Eve. Our guess is they'd still rise as a zombie after they died, but at least now with some of their higher brain functions still intact. Not controlling the body, but still there, and for much longer."**

Dr. M: "I don't even need to say what this could mean."

Resident E: "And we can't assume that this is a coincidence, finding corpses infected with a stronger strain buried in a New Biotech landfill."

Resident Z: "As a stronger virus, it might be perceived by the lesser strains as an 'Alpha,' as it were, drawing normal zombies to it."

Dr M: "Ricky? How do you respond to the idea of a stronger strain of the virus in the New Biotech landfill?"

Ricky: Look, until zombies came along New Biotech held about a 12% share of the pharmaceutical business, at best. When Athena debuted her shiny new disease on national television, we thought we were done. Several of us had no doubt that one of our bigger competitors would have a cure or vaccine or delaying treatment in six months. But nobody did. Nobody came close. Then I showed up and took us in a whole different direction. Instead of fighting it, I suggested riding with it. Zombies as test subjects, new marketing campaign for cosmetics, but you know all that already.

Dr. M: "Yes, we do."

Ricky: So like I mentioned before, I had enemies, and some of those enemies – primarily that lame ass Dudley – wanted to see the company succeed in some way that at the same time cut me down. Ideally because I wouldn't be a part of the success.

Dr. M: "Other parts of the company continued the vaccine research."

Ricky: So it would appear.

Dr. M: "So why keep it a secret? Why hasn't New Biotech released this new strain to the general public?"

Ricky: Your boy said it already. It's contagious. No exclusive rights. We've spent the gross national product of a small country on a cure for this thing. Give it to one person the way it is now and they just pass it on through sex for free or selling their blood on the street. New Biotech isn't going to let this out until they can make their money back and a thirty percent margin on top of that.

Dr. M: "So, just to be clear, you're saying that New Biotech is content to let the zombie plague propagate across the planet, even when they potentially have a way to release a much more powerful, yet much less harmful strain, which would not kill people?"

Ricky: Any idea what sort of bonus goes with a thirty percent margin?

Dr. M: "Zach, Eve, did we get enough of the new strain on our equipment to replicate it?"

Resident Z: "Oh, no way. I didn't even consider that until three days in the lab. By then it was long dead."

Dr. M: "Then we need more."

Resident E: "Already thought of that."

Resident Z: "What? When?"

Resident E: "Just a minute ago, but I was waiting for everyone to catch up."

Dr. M: "Share, please."

Resident E: "We break in to New Biotech."

Resident Z: "I'm sorry, I thought I heard you just say, 'Break in.'"

Dr. M: "I'm sure she means walk in, in broad daylight. Get a few files, maybe a sample, and then leave, right?"

> **Ricky:** Get in, maybe. Get on a computer, highly doubtful. Get a sample, no way.

Resident E: "Well, obviously we can't trust Corporate Lackey-boy here. But I think we still have a chance."

Ricky: What makes you think you have any sort of hope?

Resident E: "Because we also have Marie."

Dr. M: "Ah! Her friend's daughter got in once long enough to infect an entire floor and sneak out again. Is she still around?"

Resident Z: "Are we seriously talking about this?"

Dr. M: "Zach, did you miss the earlier part of the conversation?"

Resident E: "I'll talk to Marie, see if she knows where her friend's daughter is or can tell us how to get in, either way."

Resident Z: "Dr. Marshall, we're getting way out of our league here. What happened to studying the zombie experience? What happened to documenting change from one mental state to another? That's what we signed up to do. That's why we're here. That's what the grant money pays for."

Dr. M: "Zach, I understand your concerns. Our work isn't going away. Even if this new strain does what we think it does, we're still going to have zombies, and lots of them. But the point is, we could offer the people of the world a chance to live full and productive lives before becoming zombies. For that matter, opportunities for continued development long after their bodies have failed and thanks to our research, ways to communicate with them."

Resident Z: "I'm not going outside of my field. I'm here for a very specific part of this research, and that's it."

Dr. M: "No one is asking you to do anything else, Zach. If we decide to go this route, and we haven't decided that yet, all participation will be strictly voluntary. Okay?"

Resident Z: "Okay."

Dr. M: "I think we've gone as far as we need to today. Eve, let me know what you find out, everyone else, thanks."

Day 68

(Resident Eve Notes: Dr. Marshall met me and Zach in the break room today while we were eating lunch. Since we rarely eat lunch together – in fact, that may have been the first time – I noted it as odd, but no one said anything about it. Midway through, Dr. Marshall got up and picked up a pen in front of a dry-erase board on the wall. I had a digital hand-held recorder on me, and since I had a long history of note-taking or recordings, Dr. Marshall didn't seem to mind.)

"I want a back-up plan," he said with no introduction.

"To what?" Zach kept eating as he spoke, a tuna-fish sandwich with onions as I recall.

"Getting the super strain from New Biotech."

When he spoke I glanced around the room to make sure no one was listening. The only other person was an intern on her way out the door.

"Sir, we've already located the daughter of Marie's friend, Mrs. Bradford, and she's on board. We're figuring out a way to wire her the money now." What I said was mostly true. We still had to come up with a plan to break into a highly secure corporate office and then explain it to her, plus make a few other technical arrangements.

"Right." Dr. Marshall looked at me. "Are you going with her?"

I hesitated. "I… suppose I could. At least to the New Biotech building lobby."

"Again I ask everyone to step back and reconsider this." Zach smacked his sandwich as he spoke. It made my stomach turn a little.

"I think Ricky was probably telling the truth." Dr. Marshall couldn't seem to decide what to write on the dry-erase board. He fidgeted a little bit, still holding the marker. "This probably is a doomed mission. If we're sending someone into something like that, they should at least have someone they can call when things go wrong."

"Sure, I wouldn't mind doing that." I said those words, but I lied them. More travel meant more hopping between airfields we hoped hadn't been overrun since the last updates. Plus the last time I encountered New Biotech they chased me away with helicopters armed with chain guns.

"Is that it?" I noticed Zach had some tuna in his beard, and I tried not to stare as he spoke.

"No, obviously. If we think that's going to fail, we need to be working something else in the background." Dr. Marshall took the cap off the marker, then put it back on again. "I know the sample we have is a dead one, but Zach I want you to see what you can do to replicate it anyway."

"How exactly?"

"I don't know. Clone it. Pull out its DNA and shoot it in a live virus. Something."

"I'm not a virologist or a geneticist, nor do I know any, nor am I sure I've ever met any."

Dr. Marshall seemed frustrated. "Do you think you could find some? Offer to put them on staff for a few weeks? Hell, I'll take a handful of grad students at this point."

"We don't have any budget for that." Zach wiped his face with a napkin, completely missing that one piece of tuna in his scraggly face hair. "And if we did, the process to hire someone for this sort of work would take at least a month."

"I'm not sure we have a month."

"Before they take Ricky?" I asked. "Who cares? He's a jerk anyway. Even for a zombie."

Dr. Marshall looked at me with calmer eyes, and it dawned on me what he was saying.

"You're worried about Sigourney." I said it out loud for Zach's benefit. Dr. Marshall nodded and we were all quiet for a moment.

"You think less than a month?" Zach asked.

"On the one hand, she's good at suppressing the degeneration, at least outwardly." Dr. Marshall put the pen down on the table. "I don't think she realizes I can see emotional spikes that big on the decoder."

I'd reviewed the transcripts of Sigourney's session with Jonathan again that morning. Reading it you could almost imagine you weren't listening in on two dead people.

"I'll see what I can do, but seriously, I've got no contacts in this area." Zach's tone changed to the one he used whenever he was thinking about something else, which I took as a good sign.

"If nothing else, see if Richelle knows… knew anybody that might still be out there." Dr. Marshall looked down at the ground for a few seconds before continuing. "I'll work on a back-up to the back-up plan. There are still a few things I want to check out."

And that's more or less where the conversation ended. It left me feeling generally anxious. Whatever the original point of our research, a strain of the virus which protected people from turning, or at least delayed it, would change the entire zombie problem. It seemed obvious that Dr. Marshall carried the weight of that potential, or more to the point, the possibility of letting that potential slip through his fingers. I resolved to show more enthusiasm about my part in the plan—around him anyway.

Day 70

(Resident Eve Notes: Once we finally settled on doing it, adjusting the Group Therapy set-up so it functioned as a Dayroom wasn't that difficult. We had to drastically increase the storage capacity for a lot more recording, but Zach solved that with a trigger switch. The switch didn't log intermittent emotions or images of anyone in the Dayroom, but only captured whenever they actually spoke. In addition, we gave everyone two two-word combinations ("[Name] Dayroom" and "[Name] Exit") which allowed them to enter and leave the social area at will, based on their individual comfort levels. Teaching them all how to use the new method only took a few hours, and we rigged a "bell" to ring in their heads to notify them whenever the Dayroom was officially open. To offer a feeling of privacy, I had Zach install "record" and "stop record" code words as well, my reasoning being that if they knew they could interact privately, that might help pull some of their inner issues out for discussion later. We set up the first run to go overnight, and it went unsupervised to see how they would react without their primary care team nearby. Not surprisingly, on the first day open for business, the two youngest members of the group, Tom and Lisa, were the first to test the waters.)

Tom (Imitating echo): HELLO? Hello? Hello?

Lisa: Blah, blah. Are we the only ones here?

Tom: Yeah, I think so.

Lisa: Oh.

(Resident Eve Notes: Both subjects were quiet for approximately two minutes.)

Lisa: What was your name again?

Tom: Tom.

Lisa: High school. Right.

Tom: Right.

Lisa: Yeah.

Ricky: Hey, am I late?

Lisa: Oh, thank God.

Sam: I'm in.

Janis: Janis here.

Dead Eddie: Hey Gray Eyes! Hey… everyone else.

Richelle: This should be interesting.

(Resident Eve Notes: A minute and a half passed in silence.)

Ricky: Think anyone else is coming? Looks like a no-show for Sigourney, Denial Boy, and What's-her-face the religious nut.

Dead Eddie: Screw 'em.

Richelle: I may have spoken too soon.

Ricky: Richelle! I'm really glad you made it especially.

Richelle: Why's that?

Ricky: I was hoping you could help us get this party really going.

Lisa: Party? How party?

Richelle: Why would we want… what sort of party?

Ricky: Well, that was some great work you did with Zach and Eve and the whole super-virus- gives-more-oxygen thing.

Richelle: Thanks, but I'm not sure we're supposed to talk about it. Also, not sure how that relates to a party.

Ricky: So I got to wondering just how much help you actually did with that whole thing.

Richelle: What do you mean? I had quite a part in the research, thank you.

Ricky: How? I mean, you can't exactly get up and stand at a microscope.

Richelle: No, but I had access to all the pictures, and graphs. I still understood those.

Ricky: Access? Do tell.

Richelle: They gave me some code words to get to Zach's files and I would call them up and…

Ricky: Exactly!

Richelle: Exactly what? You're confusing me.

Ricky: You can get to their files!

Richelle: Well, sure, but you already know everything…

Ricky: Not those files, the *real* files. The files about *us*.

Richelle: Oh, I don't think we should go digging around in those.

Ricky: Oh, I do.

Sam: Richelle, if I may. I don't normally go along with Ricky, but I must say that it is a tried and true fact that whenever enough whack jobs get together in one psychiatrical-type location, they always manage to somehow break out and get the copies of their records.

Richelle: Really?

Sam: Absolutely. Either that or they go to a public sporting event somewhere. Since we can't walk, that leaves the files-reading option. It may possibly even be a moral imperative.

Ricky: What else do we have to do with our time?

Sam: I think it usually involves forgotten tunnels and flash-lights, though. Possibly bribing one of the night watchmen with booze.

Ricky: So Richelle, what do you say?

(Resident Eve Notes: Once Richelle agreed, what followed was an hour long attempt between Richelle and Ricky to figure out how to navigate around on Zach's server. Since the system only responded to Richelle's inputs, but she couldn't read, their time passed mostly in a comedy of errors. Richelle would give a command, describe what she saw, then Ricky would have her "pull" that image to the group. He would read it, and then tell her what command to try next. While fascinating in its own right, I've saved that interaction on another file for problem-solving research, but deleted it from this record.)

Ricky: We're in! All right, let's see what we've got here.

Sam: The suspense is terrible. I hope it lasts.

Richelle: Are all those files on us?

Ricky: You got it. Let's see, it starts with an overview about how we all have, quote, "feelings of unreality, and that their bodies do not belong to them, and in some cases subjects act as if in a dreamlike state."

Sam: Boring.

Ricky: Plus, duh.

Janis: Get to the personal stuff.

Ricky: All right. We don't have a Tom do we? Do we have a Tom?

Tom: That's me.

Ricky: Tom! You go first. "Failure to conform to society's norms and expectations plus impulsiveness present in failure to consider consequences of behaviors."

Tom: That's what I said, I'm in high school.

Ricky: Right. Next. Lisa. "Biological needs crosswiring combined with an extreme difficulty in controlling sexual impulses despite the negative consequences."

Lisa: Hello? College student.

Ricky: Another good point. I wonder how much we're paying these guys?

Janis: What does it say for you, Ricky?

Ricky: For me it says, "Disregard for the rights of others. Symptoms of Narcissistic Personality Disorder." AKA Corporate Mogul. Let's move on.

Dead Eddie: How about me, Gray?

Ricky: Let's see, Dead Eddie. "falsely believes that insignificant remarks, events, or objects in his environment have personal meaning or significance, namely the specific movements and actions of the great northeastern hordes as well as the leadership qualities of a delusional character called Old Gray Eyes."

Dead Eddie: Why do they think you're delusional?

Lisa: These aren't very flattering. I mean, I could control my impulses if I wanted to.

Janis: We're all sure you could.

Sam: No doubt.

Ricky: Jonathan, also delusional, of the "somatic" variety, whatever that means. "believes his body has not changed…" Oh, the list goes on and on, people! Can you believe what they're saying about us? I mean, who are they to judge us?

Janis: What does NOS mean? Mine says, "Delusional NOS."

Sigourney: It means "Not Otherwise Specified." Ricky, what are you doing?

Ricky: Sigourney! I didn't think you were coming. Maybe you could warn us or something, next time.

Sigourney: I'll be sure to do that. What are you doing?

Ricky: We're looking at our records. Want to see yours?

Sigourney: No, I most distinctly do not and I don't think you should, either. Richelle, can you shut this down?

Ricky: Hey there, hold on.

Richelle: I'm not sure how.

Sigourney: You all understand we're being recorded, right? Dr. Marshall is going to be very disappointed in you.

Lisa: I thought Eve said we could turn the recordings on and off.

Sigourney: Did anyone actually turn the recordings off?

(Resident Eve Notes: A few seconds of silence passed.)

Ricky: Oh, now we're really going to get it.

Richelle: What? No! I was just helping with research... I didn't... Richelle exit!

(Resident Eve Notes: After Richelle left, the link to the files and records went with her, severing contact with Zach's server.)

Tom: Tom exit.

Ricky: Wimps.

Dead Eddie: I'm still here, Gray.

Ricky: Of course you are.

Janis: I actually really don't have anything else to do with my time.

Sam: What she said.

Sigourney: I'm leaving. Sigourney exit.

(Resident Eve Notes: A few more seconds of silence passed.)

Lisa: Well, now what are we going to do?

Ricky: So we can turn the machines on and off now?

Janis: That's what the nice doctor said.

Ricky: I've got an idea of something fun we can do, if you all are up for it.

Lisa: So many nights start this way… Started, this way.

Janis: Why not?

Ricky: Stop recording.

(Resident Eve Notes: The Dayroom equipment fell silent after that, and resumed recording approximately an hour later. Apparently Ricky came up with the idea to use the "stop" and "start" feature as a way to edit together a "show" they performed as a group.

I didn't play back the recordings until the next day. After I'd reviewed the data and reported it to Dr. Marshall, he of course ordered me to pull the "dayroom" plug at once and keep it that way indefinitely. Zach disabled the word activation codes for his server the same afternoon. I think under normal circumstances Dr. Marshall would have brought the group together for

some sort of verbal admonishment, but his preoccupation with the super-strain of the Athena virus took a higher priority. He said the group participants would know that what they did was both unethical and a violation of trust, and they could each stew on those thoughts without his help.

Dr. Marshall didn't seem remotely interested in the "show," and stopped watching after the first fifteen seconds. The implications of patients reading their own records far overshadowed what amounted to a juvenile production number afterwards. Zach and I reviewed the entire program, and I've included it in the interest of complete documentation. For continuity sake, I removed all the "Stop recording" commands.)

Ricky: Hello everyone, welcome back. My name is Ricky and I've been elected by the group to be tonight's voiceover narrator.

Sam: We couldn't get Morgan Freeman.

Lisa: Oh my God, is he a zombie?

Janis: No, dear.

Lisa: I bet he'd be yummy.

Janis: Shush.

Ricky: And while I'll be doing the speaking, I'd like to stop now and thank Sam and Janis, who wrote tonight's script…

Sam: Thank you, thank you.

Janis: Thanks.

Ricky: …and to thank Lisa and Dead Eddie, who will be providing most of the additional ambiance for the program. So, without further delay… let's begin…

(Resident Eve Notes: They kept recording here for a minute, but no one said anything. I believe this was Ricky's way of "fading in" from black.)

Dead Eddie: Ahem. Chirp. Chirp, chirp.

Ricky: As the fog settles over the still burning car husks, across the wind-swept empty streets, a stunning unnatural wonder unfolds…

Lisa: Aaaah. Smack, smack.

Ricky: While she awakens, she will not sleep again, while she reaches and claws at others, she cannot feel… Mostly, she will shamble, but she won't shamble alone… She will pursue her singular purpose, which we examine tonight, in…

The Unnatural World…

Dead Eddie: Bum bum bum bum bum! Bum-diddy bum bum, da de da bum-diddy bum bum...

Ricky: Adversity surrounds her from the beginning. Her limbs, twisted, possibly missing. Her senses confused, also possibly missing. Tired but filled with an endless energy for her cause, she stumbles out into the humid summer streets.

Lisa: Stumble, stumble. Blech,n blech eck.

Ricky: We don't know what she looks for in a potential coupling, we only know that she is relentlessly searching, no matter how long it takes, and we know when she's found what she desires...

Lisa: Grrrrr. Argh.

Dead Eddie: Aieeeeee!

Lisa: Crunch. Yum.

Ricky: But unlife is not easy for the common zombie. Dangers lurk behind every street corner…

Dead Eddie: Pow! Pew! Pew!

Ricky: It looks like a sniper has taken up a position in the east…

Dead Eddie: Pow! Pow!

Lisa: Grrrrr?

Ricky: Fortunately, this one has forgotten that loud noises attract other members of the horde, and doesn't realize that the pile of clothing in the corner contains the upper half of Mrs. Crabtree…

Dead Eddie: Pow! Pew! Oh no! Owwieeee! Glug glug.

Lisa: Grrrrr…

Ricky: The peril seems to have passed, for now… but what's this?

Dead Eddie: Brrrrrrrrrrrr brack-a-tat-a-tat-a-tat…

Ricky: The last remaining member of the Air Force strafes the highway from above…

Lisa: Sad grrrrr.

Ricky: The horde clusters, not for protection, but because that's what they do. A thousand arms reach up in futile gestures towards the shiny pretty object…

Dead Eddie: Br-brack-a-tat-a-tat-a-tat… Ka-Powie! Ka-Boom!

Lisa: More grrrrr.

Dead Eddie: Ka-Bloowie! Crash! BOOM! BOOM! POW!

Lisa: Bored grrrrr.

Dead Eddie: Um, pow.

Ricky: And finally, the streets silent again, the zombies con tinue, almost as one harmonious assembly. They absorb the curses tossed at them by the living from their watchtowers and second floor balconies, judged and mocked for their lack of hygiene, their particular dietary requirements, and their clothing malfunctions.

With no end in sight, she persists in her never ending quest for sustenance, and to procreate.

Lisa: Two-for-one grrrr.

Ricky: As the sun sets, she does not. Time does not wait for zombies, nor does it pause the living in order to give the undead a chance to catch up. No, they do not, cannot rest… not in this, the Unnatural World…

Dead Eddie: Bum bum buuuuuuuum!

Janis: Annnnnd, scene.

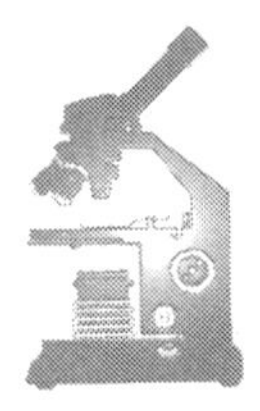

Day 75

A week after Dr. Marshall requested the "back-up plan" I met the daughter of Marie's friend on a cool fall morning at a secured airstrip in the Appalachians, a little over a hundred miles from the nearest edge of the northeastern horde. She requested I not use her name in my notes so I'll refer to her as "Lola." Lola had the look so many people on the front lines had these days, abandoning any sense of fashion for the more practical black or green utilitarian military gear. She only carried a pistol on her thigh, which led me to believe she wasn't a fighter – just someone who didn't want to be caught alone with no way to either defend herself or to put a bullet in her own head if it came down to it.

Ideally, I'd have faxed or emailed her the plan in detail, but since we didn't have a direct satellite link, the condition and the security of the few remaining networks were too unreliable. Plus, she didn't seem like she'd seen much in the way of electricity in a while, or hot water.

"I don't know how much you know," she began, "but the main New Biotech building, the original corporate headquarters, is completely abandoned." As she spoke I threw my backpack over my shoulder and she led me away from the plane. The cleanliness of my clothes announced me as a carpet-dweller to the few bodyguards, pilots and mechanics we passed along the way.

"I did not know that," I responded. I might not have needed to get on a plane at all.

"After that little outbreak I, you know, had a minor part in, it spread a lot faster than we thought it would."

"So did they move, or…?"

"They did." Lola gestured to another plane, this one even smaller and less reputable-looking, sitting on the edge of the tarmac. "The current branch office now sits on an offshore oil rig down in the Gulf."

That would explain another plane ride. No chance we'd make it all the way to the coast on the ground.

"So can we fly there?" I asked.

"Provided you can wire a few more funds to another account, I tentatively have a boat waiting for us."

"But this entire coast is..."

"Right, sorry, there aren't any airfields near any ports on this coast any more. Plane to the helicopter, helicopter to the sea, and therefore the boat, then boat to the rig. And yes, that is going to cost your organization quite a bit of dough." She turned at me and smiled. "You get me for free, though, ammo included."

For the first hour of the plane ride we talked very little other than to review the plan whenever we were sure the pilot couldn't overhear us. Corporations still had money, for whatever money was worth, and they loved buying information as much as desperate survivors loved selling it. After we were relatively confident we knew what we were doing, we both relaxed, and being too tense to nap, we started idle conversation. I don't remember a lot of it. We talked about where we grew up and went to school and some of the softer world news, that sort of thing. What I do remember is how the conversation turned after I asked how well she knew Marie.

"She's been my mom's best friend for years. I grew up thinking of her more of an aunt than anything else," she said, then looked down at her hands. "Just another casualty in the fight now."

"What about your mom? Is she… ?"

"They were in the same church." Lola said it like that explained everything, and I guess it did. She smiled at me in a sad way, and I suspected she wanted to say more. It turned out simply maintaining eye contact and not saying anything, waiting for her to be ready, was all she needed.

"I mean, when I heard them talking about infecting a bunch of corporate bigwigs I was, like, 'Right on! Sign me up!' And then I do it, right? I went in, really convinced it was going to make a difference, right? I could have been arrested, tried for manslaughter or murder, but because those guys were evil, I did it anyway."

She looked out the window for a few seconds.

"You did it anyway," I prompted. I didn't know how this related, but my therapy instincts went out on autopilot.

"And… and we shut the building down." She turned back to me. "The whole building, corporate headquarters, completely grinds to a halt. Millions, maybe billions of dollars that these guys practically bathe in, all lost. It was perfect. It was an absolute victory. They were going to have to rethink making dolls more zombie-like and commercials with subliminal pro-zombie messages, and we made them pay for all the people they converted to help run their machines. I mean, I'm not sure how it could have gotten any better."

"Well, that sounds good."

"Yeah, right? I was good." She waved her hands as she spoke. "It was good and then two weeks later she deliberately infects herself. Both of them did. As part of some freakin' religious epiphany, of all things."

"That must have been very hard for you." I resisted the urge to reach over and put a hand on her arm. It had been so long since

I'd listened to someone with a pulse, I realized I kept forgetting to think about my non-verbal signals and facial expressions as we spoke.

"No biggie. I think they both got mauled by a wandering gaggle of college students, anyway. Dead ones, obviously. I didn't really hear the details."

"I think it probably was a biggie." I turned to face her and make eye contact. "I mean, the loss of your mother and surrogate aunt at the same time? That's gotta be rough for anybody."

"I guess so." She perked up a little after that. "So, as I understand it, you're working on some way to talk to zombies?" I nodded as she spoke. "Are you able to talk to Aunt Marie?"

I hesitated before answering, wondering Lola's intent in asking. "Yes, actually we can. Is there something you'd like me to ask her or tell her when I get back?" I'm not sure what inspired me to add that last part.

She thought about it and, watching her face, I could almost hear some of the biting questions anyone would want to ask a loved one who essentially committed suicide.

In the end, Lola resisted. "No, I'm good."

I gave her a few more seconds of silence to see if she'd change her mind. When she didn't, I followed up with, "So, do you have any big plans for the future?"

"Actually, I'm thinking about joining a militia," she said. "I hear they're recruiting in Fargo."

"Really?" I asked with that tone of voice that always implies actual interest whether you feel it or not. Although in this case I did.

"I know everyone is struggling to keep the economy from completely dissolving, and keeping food and water and services going, and repopulating the human race and all that, but honestly, I just really want to kill a zombie."

"One in particular?" I joked, although the look in her eyes hinted at a kernel of truth in my question.

"No, no, I mean, I've never killed one. Not one. Almost everyone I know has killed at least one."

"I see. Well, I wish you well with that."

She studied my face. "Do you think that's horrible? I mean, you're trying to talk to them, right? Study them? Do you even think they're evil?"

I'd never expected to be asked that question so directly. "Well," I paused, "I think inside, they are still what they were before, whatever that was."

"But on the outside they're rabid animals," she said in a sharp tone. "They do terrible things, and they need to be put down." She sat back in her chair, no longer looking at me. "I don't care what they were before."

After that, small talk ended, and we only spoke if one of us had a question about the plan for getting into New Biotech. The plan, if you could call it that, consisted of me waiting on the boat while Lola used a fake ID to get into the office. After that, she was on her own to steal as much as she could, be it data files or actual vials filled with super-strain virus. I brought along a small camera and microphone transmitter I put in her hair so at a bare minimum she could transmit anything she saw or read. Even if they caught her and searched her and threw her out, any computer screens she walked passed might give us something.

Excluded from the plan was any sort of food or lodging arrangement along the way. I took Lola's lead and after the first hour slept wherever I could. I did notice that each time we stopped she startled awake and checked her gun. I guess we were safe in the air, but two women traveling alone did need to make sure we were landing where we said we wanted to go and not someplace where we might become commodities in the black market. I'd packed a bag of crackers for snacks and some bottles of water, but hadn't counted on this long a trip. Fortunately Lola had several cans of peaches and beans in her bag and let me share them with her. We both ignored the expiration dates on the labels.

The biggest part of the project for me involved taking Lola's picture, printing it out on a small hand-held printer, and getting it on to the fake ID Zach designed before I left. That kept me busy most of the boat ride. Fortunately Zach made several copies for when I screwed up the first two, but trying to read and work on something that small while moving in the open sea also made me nauseated towards the end.

"Okay, and for the next sixty minutes your name is?" I asked her while adjusting the camera and microphone in her hair.

"Dawn Leibowitz," she said, clearly uncomfortable in the dress clothes I'd brought for her. Especially without her pistol.

"And you do what?"

"I'm an administrative assistant," she replied.

"For whom?"

"My first answer is 'Why is that important?' but if they push it for anything related to security issues, I work in the legal department for Augustus [name redacted]."

"Good enough. And what's the safe word?" I admit I felt vaguely excited about all this cloak-and-dagger talk. Especially since I would be back secure in the boat, doing none of the actually cloak-and -dagger work.

"Puppies. I say it, that means I'm busted and you need to either help me or leave, preferably help me."

"If I can I will, but I have no idea how." That was true on both counts. If I left I wouldn't even know where to tell the boat captain to go, and he'd go somewhere at the first sign of trouble no matter what I told him. I also hadn't touched a gun since the classes they made everyone take in school.

A New Biotech security ship met us about a half-mile from the oil rig. With the one cargo crane, from that distance the whole thing looked like a massive squatting elephant with a skin of metal lacework. One guy on the other ship manned some sort of machine gun swiveling on a poorly welded post, while another leaned over the side to check us out. Lola showed her ID while the boat captain and I claimed we were the hired transportation. That was enough to get us escorted to the rig. The real security, we knew, would be at the top of the rusted elevator.

We waited at the line of other boats waiting to drop off people and thirty minutes passed with no one speaking. I did my best to look impassive as Lola slowly ascended up into the web of white and orange-brown pipes and beams. As our boat pulled away I went down below deck to check the transmission. It worked, although all the metal interfered more than I'd thought it would.

Through the camera feed it seemed like Lola blended in just fine. We'd timed it right, a little after the initial rush of people to work. She'd seem late but not enough to generate any real questions. As she got closer I noticed that everyone else wore their badges on a lanyard around their necks and I had pinned Lola's to her collar. A small point, but it wouldn't take too much sticking out before they started to suspect something was off about her.

As she waited in line at the metal detector, the sniffer dogs alerted on someone up ahead. Everyone else, and eventually Lola, took a knee as more guards rushed in and dragged some pale poor bastard screaming off into an adjacent room. He was either a mule for drugs, or he was infected. Either way I guessed the outcome would most likely be the same for him.

The good news was, that event reduced the number of security personnel actually working the scanners. The bad news was, the ones still working seemed wide-eyed and hyper-alert after that. The group at the metal detector slowed as well, each person wanting to make sure they didn't do anything that would trigger a false alarm.

Finally Lola made it through the detector with no more of a visual inspection than the man in front of her. The sniffer dogs, too, paid her no attention. I actually felt my pulse speed up when she passed the dogs, and it really spiked when she swiped her ID card at the door and the light turned yellow with a modest but angry buzz instead of green with a friendly beep. She swiped it again, same thing. The audio picked up a derogatory comment from someone behind her. She swiped it one more time, and I saw a uniformed wrist come into frame and touch her lightly on the arm.

"Could I see you over here for a second?" the security guard said in a pleasant voice. Lola followed him over to his desk where he sat next to a computer screen.

"I think I might have bent it yesterday on the way home," Lola's voice said. Good one.

The guard smiled and held out his hand. "Well, let me see your card and I'll see if we can fix that." Lola's hand passed the card to him and he slapped it into a slot on the keyboard.

"Ms. Leibowitz?" he asked, studying the screen.

"That's me."

"Did anyone talk to you yesterday? Your boss mention anything?"

"No." Lola's voice shook a little as she spoke. "I wasn't feeling well – normal reasons, nothing weird – and didn't come back after lunch, why?"

The guard took her card out and set it on the desk near his hand, but out of reach for Lola. "I hate to be the one to tell you this, but my records show you've been let go."

"Really? Well, that's less than ideal. Are you sure?"

"Yeah, it's pretty clear here on my screen." He pointed to the screen Lola couldn't see. "And that happens sometimes. I mean, no one mentioned a round of layoffs yesterday, but they always have to put those in weeks in advance and sometimes the person isn't around the day it is scheduled to happen."

"I see," Lola replied. "Does it say it happened yesterday?"

"No, it doesn't give a day, just notice that you used to work here and now you don't."

"Hurm. Well, this is awkward, isn't it?"

"Sorry." He shrugged trying to combine friendliness and sympathy in a single motion.

Ten minutes later, she was back on the boat.

"I could come back as a vendor, or maybe even a customer." Lola paced angrily as the boat headed back to the helicopter rendezvous spot. "I'd have to be international, but I could probably fake that."

She went on like this for awhile before I spoke up.

"Lola, I think we're just going to have to call this one, okay?"

"What, you mean we're done?" She crossed her arms and glared at me.

"Look, I'm a scientist, a brain scientist at that. We're not secret agents, we're not superheroes." I didn't want to tell her what I really thought. "Besides, we're way over budget as it is."

"I have some money," she said.

"One of these boat trips alone would eat up anything you have saved."

Finally she agreed and we went the rest of the trip back in silence. We couldn't talk over the roar of the helicopter either, and she left with a terse handshake once we landed at the airfield. She didn't know that we'd created that fake employee ID in the New Biotech database. There was no way she could be really fired since she didn't exist. Someone had to have gone in and deliberately manipulated the fake files we had just created so we would be stopped, but also not taken into custody. Nothing that deliberate went by without a lot of thought. By now whoever did it had her picture on file and flagged for facial recognition. The truth was I didn't want to endanger Lola again. They let us go, once. I didn't want to take my chances with a second time.

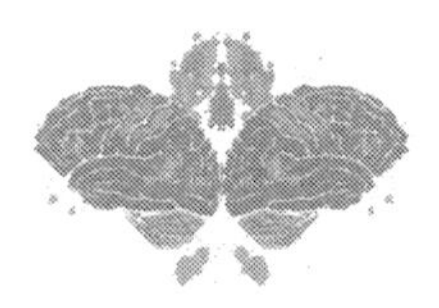

Day 81

(Resident Eve Notes: The plane rides back seemed to take a lot longer than the original flights. Part of that I'm sure stemmed from my body adjusting to the substandard food and sleeping conditions. Sad to say given how much better I have it than most of the people out there now. Especially those on the coasts.

After I arrived back at the office, Dr. Marshall seemed undaunted when I broke the news to him, and that affected me more than if he'd yelled, cried, or shown any amount of healthy emotion. When he spoke, his tone, his mood, they all had the energy he'd always shown when approaching a new problem. But the moment he stopped speaking, the moment I let the room fall silent, his shoulders slumped, just a little, and his eyes lost their focus. He knew more than any of us how few options, and how little time, Sigourney had left.)

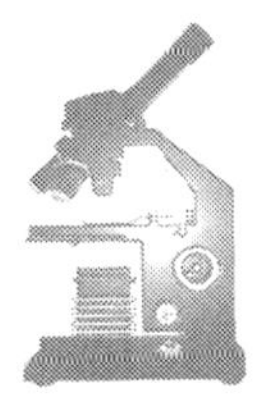

Day 82

Case Study "Sam McGee" and "Janis"

Interview #3

(Resident Eve Notes: Dr. Marshall met with the money people earlier this morning, and it is clear he's feeling the stress to show some significant progress to the outside world. He spent nearly two hours briefing a committee of six people in one of our smaller conference rooms. When they came out, their enthusiasm seemed forced, and Dr. Marshall emerged with slumped shoulders and fresh bags under his eyes.

And amid all the preparations for the public group session, a request from Sam and Janis for a meeting prodded us to continue our work. Dr. Marshall took a moment to splash some cold water on his face and grab a quick cup of coffee, and reenergized, he gathered us to join in this impromptu couples session.

Along the way, he also mentioned that he felt as though he was betraying Sigourney, not letting her listen in or know about this interview, which seemed odd given that she was in a closet less than 10 feet away. She may have been able to help

again, but with her condition such as it was, and Dr. Marshall's attention already pulled in several directions, he thought it best to focus on one thing at a time. Sam and Janis are on week 2 of being hooked up to each other 14 hours a day, with a 10 hour automated "rest" period apart from each other every night.)

Dr. M: "So what's going on with you two today?"

Sam: First off, I'm only here because if I didn't come she wouldn't come.

(Resident Eve Notes: Dr. Marshall muted the microphone and told me that he considered ending the session right then and there, and in retrospect maybe he should have. Despite his burst of enthusiasm from a few moments earlier, he said he wasn't sure he had the mental energy for this sort of encounter, and perhaps they would be better suited if Resident Zach handled it. I suspected that he might have been subconsciously wanting to punish Zach, as Dr. Marshall clearly did harbor a certain amount of resentment towards Zach's attitude. More than once I'd heard him say that Zach just didn't seem to care about the task he'd been given. I'm sure, though, that Dr. Marshall would have been happy to admit he was wrong rather than gain a pyrrhic "I told you so" at the cost of another patient. I mention these thoughts because they distracted me during the interview with Sam and Janis. I have no idea how they affected Dr. Marshall, but after he decided to proceed, he did seem preoccupied as well, almost speaking on mental cruise control. After working those issues out for a few seconds in my own mind, I was able to suppress them until the interview ended.)

Janis: Every since you hooked us up together, we talk, and it doesn't really matter now, but there are just a few things I wanted to clear up, is all.

Sam: Most of which happened so long ago I've completely forgotten about them.

Dr. M: "Let's take this a step at a time. Janis, why don't you go ahead and tell us the biggest thing that is bothering you."

Janis: When we first turned, it was almost about the same time. Within a day of each other, actually.

Sam: Just over a day.

Janis: Although you did turn first.

Sam: Men always turn first, we have faster metabolisms.

Janis: Anyway, we always traveled together after that, of course, and whenever we stumbled across an unwary victim, we used to share them.

Sam: We each liked different parts.

Janis: But after a few months, things changed. I mean, I'd be holding someone down and he'd be banging down a door that a completely different person was hiding behind. Or worse yet, he'd sneak off and finish off half a passed out vagrant and never even let out a moan to let anyone else know.

Sam: Do we have to talk about that? There is another person listening, you know.

Janis: But we used to share everything.

Sam: Look, sometimes I just wanted to have something that was my own, you know?

Dr. M: "When one person of a couple loses interest in, well, something both members used to enjoy, it can be a very traumatic time."

Janis: Then I started thinking about how far back that went. How long he'd been interested in, you know, having something that was "his own." What else might be related to that, you know?

Sam: See, here's where we hit the crazy talk.

Dr. M: "Sam, please. Let's hear what Janis has to say."

Janis: Clearly we infected each other, you know, during sex. We were married. We'd obviously been having sex for years.

Dr. M: "Go on."

Janis: Well, we never really worked out who gave it to who. And that seems like a really big deal.

Sam: Right, because as two talking corpses, somehow it matters what happened back when we had breathing bodies… And of course, if I argue with it, that automatically makes me the guilty one.

Janis: You stopped moaning at me. When you found that unprotected cellar entrance, or the downed helicopter nearby, or those elderly twins, no moans. Nothing.

Sam: You'd lost your whole left arm. I didn't want anyone to get away because you couldn't grab them properly.

Janis: That wasn't my fault.

Dr. M: "When a partner's body changes, it can be a very sensitive issue."

Janis: And even now, he keeps wanting to rehearse new material. Like we're ever going to perform again.

Dr. M: "Ah. Let's focus on that for a moment. Clearly you both enjoyed performing when you were alive. What would be the harm in practicing an activity from when you first got together?"

Sam: I keep saying that.

Janis: But what's the point? Really?

Dr. M: "It isn't like no one can ever hear you again. I can hear you now. You helped Ricky write that show you did in the Day-room."

Janis: You think… are you saying we might be able to perform somewhere again?

Dr. M: "I can't promise you anything for sure, Janis, but I will make an effort to keep an eye out for an opportunity."

Janis: Really, you'd do that for us?

Dr. M: "Again, no promises, but I'll see what I can do."

Sam: Sweet.

Janis: That would be wonderful.

Dr. M: "In the meantime, I'm going to see if we can install a more voluntary link between the two of you. Still with the auto-timer at night, but I want to make sure neither of you feels trapped. We'll add a button so you can call each other, choose to answer, choose to sever the link, etc. starting first thing to-morrow."

(Resident Eve Notes: Clearly Sam and Janis had deeper issues than just wanting more quality time together, but we thought it made a good distraction for them before Dr. Marshall decided on a more long-term course of action. We also suspected that all future such links should include an on-off switch, and then I made another note to myself to pursue some sort of network between all the subjects. Not the Dayroom or Group Therapy set up from before, but a series of private links without necessarily a collective 'common' area, and some type of switch that the subjects could manipulate to determine who they could talk to and who they would listen to. We probably wouldn't have the funds to implement or even spec out something like that until the beginning of the new quarter, but having something of a more novel nature might help boost morale within the team, particularly if the members continued to deteriorate and eventually… had to leave the group, as it were. I also added that given the situation with Sigourney, I, for one, could certainly use a boost in morale, and Dr. Marshall looked like he could use one too.)

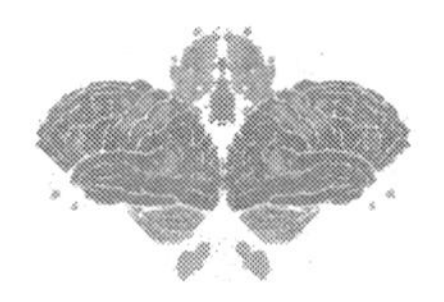

Day 87

(Resident Eve Notes: I was in Dr. Marshall's office today discussing the specifics on an idea he had for linking all the subjects together when Zach interrupted. This is the conversation to the best of my recollection.)

"Got a sec?" Zach seemed frustrated.

"Actually, we're in the middle of something," Dr. Marshall replied.

"Look, we need to talk about this whole 'super strain' thing."

Dr. Marshall's expression notably fell. "What do you mean?"

"It's taking up too much of my time and I really don't think it's going anywhere."

Dr. Marshall sat quietly for a moment so I chimed in. "How far have you gotten? Who all has agreed to work with us?"

Zach sighed, glanced at a nearby chair but didn't sit in it.

"No one really. Actually, no one at all." He seemed to struggle between not caring and expressing even more frustration at a lot of failed work. "And frankly, I don't have the bandwidth to keep doing nothing but filtering through a bunch of rejections from my peers."

"What do you think we're trying to do here?" Dr. M.'s voice cut sharp, in a tone I'd never heard from him before.

"We're developing new communication methods," Zach replied, suppressing any outward show of emotion. "We're examining the effects of NADs on memory and also for some reason we've added a whole touchy feely component that…"

"Okay, I get it!" More bite, but worse.

"Look, I've put a lot of work into this but…"

"Fine, fine, fine." Dr. Marshall wasn't even looking at Zach. "You're just a neurologist. Nothing more. Asking you to do anything else is too hard. I got it."

"I see, and how does that make you feel?" I flinched at Zach's sarcasm and waited for a reply from Dr. Marshall that never came.

Zach stood in silence for a few seconds and then turned and left. Dr. Marshall only wasted a moment staring off at nothing before he started rummaging through the drawers of his desk.

"Did you want to continue?" I asked.

"Mm?" His head didn't rise up from behind the desk. "Oh yeah, sure, in a minute."

I waited while he went through everything in every drawer of his desk and then moved on to the single overcrowded bookshelf behind him. He finally found what he was looking for on a pile sitting on top of his printer. As he sat he tossed a copy of *Undead Like Me* on the desktop. I looked at it but didn't move.

"At last count, there were only seven working printing presses left in the entire world, and only two in this hemisphere." He said it like the whole world had intentionally gone green instead of simply having lost the will and the personnel to pursue much beyond survival and military training. Not to mention the risks of logging and the evacuation of most major metropolitan areas.

"Two years ago, I got a handful of requests from Sigourney asking me to write the forward, but I didn't know who she was. Just some hack journalist," he continued. "So I turned her down once, ignored all the other messages she sent, and then promptly forgot about her.

"Eight months later a friend sent me a digital copy, and it took me five weeks to get around to opening the file and then reading it." He stared at the book while he spoke. He seemed to be speaking more to the book than to me. "And then I read it again. Then I spent half a month's rent on an actual printed copy in what I can only attribute to a moment of impulse and admiration. I suppose guilt was also a possibility."

"Uh-hm." After saying that, I realized that whenever faced with someone who obviously wanted to disclose something significant, I automatically switched over to Counseling 101 methods of prompting and making eye contact with the other person. Embarrassing, but apparently effective – even on another psychiatrist.

"I ended up quoting several passages in my first grant proposal." He kept speaking and I resisted a minimal prompt this time, waiting for him to get to what he needed to come next. "Sent my nephew to get this copy signed without revealing who he was.

"The, um… the..." His hesitation lasted longer than I would have expected. "The day before the grant review committee met was when the news came out that she'd… turned. When I called them and said I'd arranged to transfer her, in her entirety, to the Institute, it sealed the deal. They didn't come right out and say that, but, the story was so compelling..."

"Is that why you brought her here?"

"You mean for the grant money? No. No, although, I think I let a few people like Zach believe I was that level of devious." He stood up and stretched, an outward sign that he'd buried the bulk of his emotional baggage, at least temporarily. "No, just pure curiosity. That and on some level I think I admired her and her methods. When I thought about communicating with those who had turned, those for whom everyone else had given up hope… She was by far the most interesting and obvious choice."

"You know that by bringing her here you've given the public far more insight into her personality and thoughts than ever would have been possible otherwise, right?"

"Of course, of course." Dr. Marshall sat back down again and took up a pen. "Moot point now what my reasoning was. Let's move on."

And with that he jumped back to the previous small-talk topic and left it at that.

Day 89

Case Study "Sigourney"

Interview #57

(Resident Eve Notes: While the stories of Sigourney's success with Jonathan spread quickly to the other members of the group, and while that in turn boosted her morale, Sigourney's condition continued to deteriorate, in preparation for the transition to NAD Stage 4.)

MMmm, you smell good.

Dr. M: "I'm assuming you mean that in a culinary sort of way."

Assume all you want.

Dr. M: "How are you feeling today?"

Toss an intern or something my way and I'll tell you. Yeah, it won't be long now. That's how it works, isn't it? I read some of the reports from the San Francisco Center. Brain stays protected at first, then deteriorates from the outside in. Soon all I'll only be able to say stuff like HOW FREAKIN' MUCH MR. SMITHEE SMELLS LIKE BACON or stuff like that.

I did that one on purpose. Sort of.

Dr. M: "Yes, it's true. We may not have many interviews left."

All I heard was, "Blah, blah, I'm a yummy slab of meat blah."

Dr. M: "It's good you've kept your sense of humor after such a tragic turn of events."

Sure, tragic.

Dr. M: "You sound unconvinced."

Well, I spent almost a year of my life living with Reanimates. Learning their body signals, their moans, their feeding habits. There were times I had to pretend to eat with them, you know. I didn't, of course, but I still ended up with blood on my hands from time to time. And you couldn't just wipe it off on your pant legs when it was over.

You can't devote that much of your life, your mind, your emotions, to a group like the northeastern hordes and not develop some sort of a bond. I know these Reanimates, I've studied them, and on some level they know me. Gadget, the Rutger's girl, Dead Eddie…

I know, when I got bitten in Wales, it was a horrible moment. A terrible thing. But the first thing I felt when I saw the festering wound was relief. Yes, relief.

Think of it. No need to worry about aging, or death, or bodily functions of any sort. No worries with shopping, cooking, cleaning, even sleeping. You can just wander the planet, see the world, forever.

Dr. M: "Do you still see it that way?"

Well, less so now. I suspect after I transition you'll remove my torso. But I suppose you could carry me places… Maybe make a little carrying case, poke some holes in it so I could see. Or smell or hear anyway.

In the end though, I think I still made… I mean, I think it will work out.

Dr. M: "You started to say something else."

It's nothing, forget it.

Dr. M: "That bite in Wales, tell me more about it."

I don't want to talk about it. I mean…

Could I at least get you to give up a finger or something else to chew on while we talk? Or a toe? No one uses the pinky toe.

Dr. M: "You're changing the subject"

You're just going to keep asking me, aren't you? You are really frustrating some times.

(Resident Eve Notes: Dr. Marshall remained quiet for about a minute until she continued.)

Fine. During the tour, I met this couple who really liked my book. Let's call them Elizabeth and Francis. They lived on a little farm out in the country and kept a pen of Reanimates there in order to keep them from hurting themselves or others. I guess you could say they did zombie rescue work.

Every time one of the farm animals died, or they came across some errant road kill, they brought it home and tossed it over the fence. They told me that soon the Reanimates could recognize their tone of voice, and would crowd up against the fence whenever they heard them coming. Not up against the fence near where they were, but up against the fence where they always tossed over the carcasses.

I'd heard that attempts to train Reanimates had a high failure rate, but I agreed to stop by toe… toe… tasty toes… sorry, I meant stop by "to" see their farm. Along the way they explained how their little flock, as they called it, kept growing in numbers, and they were worried that eventually the fences wouldn't hold. They were very distraught with the idea of having to put some of them down.

They were a lovely couple, semi-retired, and both their kids had moved to London years earlier. Elizabeth said their children didn't approve of keeping Reanimates, but ever since their kids were gone they'd been so lonely…

They used to sit around at night just talking to them. They gave names to those they didn't know, called any sort of meat "yummy treats" for them, and gossiped to their friends and neighbors about what fun expressions or what interesting things they had done each day.

Their farm sat between these two little green hills and they had a bunch of sheep that adjusted to the Reanimate scent over time. Little Victorian-looking house, hardwood floors, big kitchen with a special section with a drain in the floor for cutting up carcasses, all very quaint.

I stayed with them for a few weeks, getting to know them, getting to know this new horde, collecting fresh road kill. Maybe it was because these Reanimates were British and had been raised "proper" and all that, but they seemed gentler than the northeastern horde.

I didn't have any of the special blood mix to smear on me to mask my scent, but it was so hard just looking at them over a fence like that. It was hard not getting down there, in the gore-soaked dust with them, you know? They were so peaceful at times, swaying back and forth, snapping quietly at my hair.

One night the couple brought out a grill and we cooked blood sausages next to the pen under the open stars. Then right before we ate, because it was a special occasion, Francis tossed one of the older sheep over the fence. We all ate dinner together, like a big family, *all* of us.

It was really nice.

Then… then one day I couldn't take it any more.

(Resident Eve Notes: Communications stopped for two minutes. We prompted with "Take what any more?" several times. On the fourth try, she responded.)

I know what the papers said. That I got careless. That I trusted them too much and didn't take the proper precautions.

Dr. M: "There was one other rumor."

The Bowden report. Yeah, I know that one. One of the last things I read before the change.

Dr. M: "Was it true?"

Hm?

Dr. M: "We're piping this directly into your brain, I know you can hear me."

Sure you can't spare just one toe?

Dr. M: "Was it true, Sigourney?"

That I "went native"?

I wouldn't put it exactly that way. I certainly didn't want any harm to come of it. And, true, I didn't really think through all of the consequences.

Dr. M: "So it is true?"

They were all just holding up their arms, you know. Like a crowd of admirers at a rock concert. Looking up at me, reaching, mouths open. I just wanted to reach down and hold their hands, deluding myself for a moment it would be something tender or non-violent. I knew better than to reach down, but…

I moved over to where the fence had been patched with chain link, and they followed me. They pressed up against the wire, trying to jam a limb through it or their mouths. And there was this one little girl Reanimate, probably six or seven years old. Half her hair was missing, but the other half still had a big red bow in it.

(Resident Eve Notes: Communications stopped again until Dr. Marshall prompted her twice more.)

She actually made eye contact with me. They don't usually do that, you know. Normally they just focus on the nearest body part. And so without really thinking about it I slipped just the tiniest bit of my left pinky finger near her mouth.

She got more than I thought she would, of course.

(Resident Eve Notes: The readings on the monitors lit up with spikes higher than I'd ever seen before. The software wasn't sure how to decode them and they came out mostly as white noise.)

I know you probably didn't want to hear all that. Wow. It really feels good to have said it though. Really good.

Dr. M: "Sigourney, let's talk about something else for a moment."

Like whether or not I regret it all? Whether or not I wanted this? Of course not, not really.

Dr. M:* *"I meant less talk about something less emotional for now."

I mean, I've always been a model citizen, for the most part. I've never done anything, you know, immoral… EXCEPT RELEASING THAT HORDE IN WALES AND DRIVING THEM LIKE CATTLE TOWARDS LONDON.

Dr. M:* *"Stay focused, Sigourney."

Um, and I've never done anything…illegal… UNLESS YOU COUNT ALL THE TIMES I SOLD ZOMBIE BLOOD WHILE DISGUISED AS A SCIENTIST.

Dr. M:* *"Stay with me, Sigourney."

AH, GIMME A BREAK.

Dr. M:* *"Sigourney? Sigourney? SIGOURNEY?!?"

(Resident Eve Notes: In a tragic but inevitable moment, Sigourney's speech remained hostile from this point forward and we were never able to reestablish contact. It is conceivably possible that instead of fighting the change, she embraced it as a coping

method to get away from having to discuss, and therefore confront, the reasoning behind her decision to be deliberately bitten. We will never know for sure. Dr. Marshall marked her file "Stage 4" and closed her case study.)

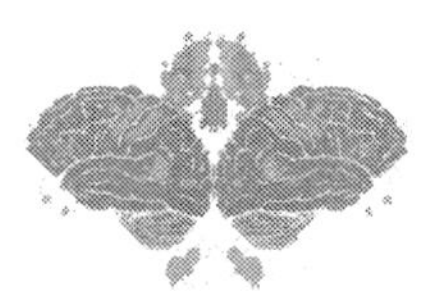

Day 91

(Resident Eve Notes: Dr. Marshall has continued his work regularly enough that I know throwing himself into his job is as least part of his coping mechanism for the loss of Sigourney.

I've tried to ask him about it, twice. In both instances he insisted that it is more important now to make a big splash within our own scientific community. The public group therapy session seemed to be the ticket to him, and he wanted to make sure everything was ready. Any time I've started him on the topic, he's mentioned either the initial article he'd written to publish and draw interest, or possibilities for public relations activities, or the most likely date for the public unveiling of our work. I supported him verbally, of course, but secretly couldn't help wonder if we just weren't ready yet. The equipment was, sure, but the subjects… They're still in the first stages of therapy. Some of them hadn't even touched on some of their deep-rooted issues. I guessed Dr. Marshall might have been counting on that, hoping to show that zombies have the same sorts of problems living people do, but it seemed like a recipe for disaster to me.

All that aside, I spent the night after we closed the Sigourney case writing up a psychological profile on Dr. Marshall for my own notes. I felt with everything else going on that he was nearing some sort of breaking point. His issues with Sigourney remained unresolved, and the stress made his body and his manner seem to age a few years every night. I thought about what might give him hope, what might help boost his spirits again, give the group some momentum, but honestly I couldn't think of anything.

I wish I'd initiated therapy with him then. I wish we'd talked about everything that was bothering him. I wish a lot of things now about that day, not a single one of which matter.)

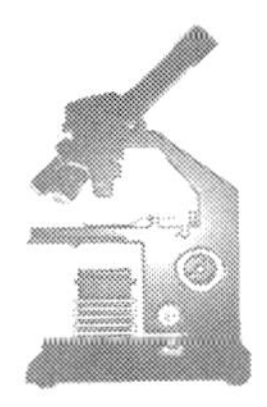

Day 92

Case Study "Group Therapy #3"

(Resident Eve Notes: Although I'm sure he'd given the matter a lot of thought, Dr. Marshall approached me rather suddenly to suggest an impromptu group session so he could break the news about Sigourney to the others.)

Dr. M: "Hello, everyone."

Janis: Hello.

Lisa: Morning, Doctor!

Ricky: How do you know if it's morning?

Lisa: It could be.

Dr. M: "I know I said our next group therapy would be public, and the one after this one will be, I promise, but I wanted to share some significant news with all of you and I thought it best if it occurred in a shared setting."

Sam: We've been cancelled, haven't we? Oh God, we've been cancelled! Did we even have a Sweeps Week?

Dr. M: "No, no, we're still functioning, as an institution anyway, and there haven't been any plans to cut funding that I know of. No, what I brought you here to discuss today is that one of our members, Sigourney, is no longer with us."

Marie: Oh, my goodness. Such a sweet girl.

Dead Eddie: Did she escape? Man, I hope she escaped.

Dr. M: "Physically, she is still here. In fact, in her same closet even. I'm afraid she's passed on to NADs Stage 4, representative of complete cognitive deterioration… She's completely bestial now, and we're no longer able to communicate with her."

Ricky: That puts a damper on the evening, doesn't it?

Lisa: How do you know if it's evening?

Ricky: It could be.

Jonathan: She was really nice to me...

Richelle: How long did she last, Doctor?

Dead Eddie: Who cares? I don't think she was really on our side, anyway.

Richelle: You should care, if you're next.

Dead Eddie: Wait. What?

Dr. M: "Richelle that's a very good point. Some of you may not have realized this, but despite the apparent near immortality of your bodies, your brain has significantly less time before you all…Well, eventually everyone here will transition to Stage 4. Eventually you'll all descend into a state most accurately described as madness, and at that moment we'll have to shut you down."

(Resident Eve Notes: The group erupted in a series of exclamations that universally expressed some feeling of surprise, anxiety, anger, or some combination of the three. They went on for several mostly incoherent minutes before Dr. Marshall was able to calm them down.)

Richelle: But Doctor Marshall, what we're working on now, this therapy we're all doing, is it going to help slow this transformation at all?

Janis: Are we curable? Well, mentally anyway…

Sam: Besides the obvious issues.

Dr. M: "There is a small chance that we can help you all learn techniques that will help delay the process, but I think you should all come to grips with the fact that it is, unfortunately, inevitable."

Ricky: So, Clyde and Richelle, could you maybe expand on that a little? For those who don't know any of the science behind all of this, and I think I speak for the majority of the group, what sort of timeline are we looking at? You've both already told me before in a private group hug, but for everyone else, what I'm trying to say is, how much time do we have?

Dr. M: "In the spirit of demystifying the process, I'd say that according to our best estimates, the average normal zombie…"

Jonathan: Reanimate.

Dr. M: "…yes, of course. According to our best estimates, the average normal Reanimate brain survives about a year before moving on to Stage 3, and then Sigourney, our first real Stage 3 subject, took several months before she went on to Stage 4."

Dead Eddie: If she's your first subject, you don't really know, do you? I mean, you're totally guessing at this point, right?

Dr. M: "The science behind it is pretty solid, Dead Eddie. What I'd like to do now is discuss what it means to all of you, to hear this news about Sigourney."

Marie: She was such a sweet girl.

Lisa: I bet you don't say that when I'm gone.

Marie: I bet I don't.

Lisa: Ouch. Sassy.

Dead Eddie: I don't plan on being in here that long. I mean, me and Old Gray, we're going places. He's got a plan. You just watch.

Ricky: Eddie, buddy, let me help you out here… I am *not* Old Gray Whoever. I have never been Old Gray Anyone, and I will never be Old Gray Anyone. It was amusing at first, but now even the obsequious sucking up is getting old.

Dead Eddie: I get it, talking too much about the plan. I'll wait until you want to bring it up some other time.

Ricky: Eddie! What are you talking about? I'm a zombie…

Jonathan: Reanimate.

Ricky: …lying motionless, on a SLAB. How much of a plan could I possibly have? I plan for the left side of me to rot a little more than the right side of me today? I plan on snapping my teeth viciously at anyone who passes within thirty feet, like I do twenty-four -seven as a matter of course? Really?

Dead Eddie: Okay, okay, I get it. Talk to you later.

Ricky: There's nothing to talk about!

Dead Eddie: Right. Okay.

Dr. M: "I'm hearing a lot of emotion, but not really the thoughts behind those emotions. Would anyone care to comment more on how they personally feel about the loss of Sigourney?"

Lisa: I miss her.

Tom: Me, too.

Dr. M: "We all miss her, Lisa, and… Tom."

(Resident Eve Notes: I'm not sure if it bears mentioning, but it was an uncharacteristic moment for Dr. Marshall to forget one of his subject's names. I think it may have been more evidence

to suggest that Sigourney's death had affected him significantly more than he cared to admit.)

Janis: I'm still stuck on this Stage 4 thing. You're essentially saying I'm going to "die" all over again, right? I mean, what's the point of even becoming a zombie?

Jonathan: Reanimate.

Sam: Jonathan, PLEASE. We appreciate how you've come to grips with your newfound non-breathingness and all, but you have GOT to stop that correcting stuff. I personally don't mind being called a zombie.

Jonathan: Reanimate.

Sam: Zombie! Zombie! Zombie! Zombie! Zombie! Zombie! Zombie! Zombie! ZOM-BIE!

Dr. M: "Sam, do you usually react this way the loss of someone near you?"

Janis: Normally he screams, "Fish stick! Fish stick! Fish stick! Fish stick! Fish stick! Fish stick!" but that hardly seems appropriate here.

Lisa: I can't believe we only have a year to live. Year and a half, tops.

Richelle: That's the *average.*

Lisa: And the world still so filled with sexy meal deals on legs... Most of them super sized…

Ricky: Of course, when you say the undead only live a year or so before changing, that's just the normal ones, right, Doc? I mean, not any of the *special* ones. Right?

Dr. M: "Ricky, let's try to stay on topic, okay?"

Janis: Special what? Special reanimates? See, that doesn't even sound right. How about super zombies?

Sam: Yeah, the other totally doesn't work.

Dr. M: "Again in the spirit of open communication, I think you all should know we've discovered what we believe is a more robust version of the virus. One that might, among other things, prolong unlife a bit, if confirmed. Finding it or replicating it being the big issue we haven't been able to solve, and the reason I haven't brought it up before."

Janis: Seriously? I thought you were making that up.

Lisa: Can we get it?

Ricky: I think they tried, or are trying, they weren't very clear on the details to me. How's that working out for you, Clyde?

Dr. M: "Like I said, we're still working to find or replicate the super strain of the virus, and I promise you that we will keep trying."

(Resident Eve Notes: At this point Dr. Marshall took off his glasses and rubbed his eyes, from my point of view, exhausted.)

Dr. M: "However, for tonight, I think maybe we all need some time to ourselves to think about how this affects us. I'm going to go ahead and end the session early, and we can bring it up again during our next group. Thank you all again for your time."

(Resident Eve Notes: While it seemed clear that the sudden awareness, or at least, the sudden attention to their own mortality caused feelings of general anxiety in all or most of the subjects, I think Dr. Marshall made a wise decision stopping there, as I doubt he could have gone on much longer and done anyone in the group any service.)

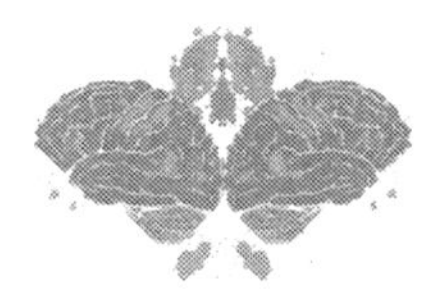

Day 93

(Resident Eve Notes: This conversation occurred during some routine maintenance Zach did every week on the neural contacts and the lab in general. I usually volunteered to help him since I found the lab filled with silent "sleeping" subjects a bit disconcerting at night whenever I was in it alone, and figured he could use the company. I recreated the conversation from memory as best as I could.)

Zach grimaced a little as he pulled the probes off the wires and put them on the sterilization cart. "Oh, I can see the letter now. Dearest Father, sorry I'm so late in writing, I got caught up wiping zombie brain matter off little pieces of metal all night long."

"Well, could be worse." Since this was all technically his job, I'd chosen the easier tasks related to software maintenance and power supply tests. "You could have to explain digging a head out of dirt."

"True, that would be harder. Or you would have to describe trying to break into an oil rig to steal zombie virus."

"Explain to whom?" I wasn't hurt by the question itself, but it did annoy me from time to time that Zach never seemed to remember I'd lost my entire family.

"Oh, right, sorry."

We worked quietly for a moment, not so much that the awkwardness had left us unable to keep speaking, but because we generally had little to talk about in the first place, and any speed bump like that drained what small amount of energy we had to spend on each other. I had one power supply that kept chirping with odd readings anyway, and three different passes through the test stand couldn't diagnose the problem. The desire not to be forced to ask Zach for help kept me focused and occupied until I finally figured out I hooked up two of the leads backwards. That would have been embarrassing to admit.

"Speaking of which," he asked a few minutes later, "how are you doing?"

"You're a neurologist and a computer geek, Zach," I teased. "I thought you didn't believe in psychoanalysis."

"Well, I didn't ask how that made you feel, did I?"

"No, you didn't." I'd noted that Zach did tend to use that phrase as a way to mock psychology in general. "And I thank you for that and for asking." I started a test sequence with a new power supply and let it run. "For the most part, I'm fine. I mean, I know Dr. Marshall took Sigourney's… well, he took the loss of Sigourney pretty hard."

"I was asking about you." Zach worked without turning towards me.

"Since you brought it up, knowing my failure at the oil rig directly led to Sigourney's loss, which in turn directly led to emotional distress in Dr. Marshall, I am having some trouble with that." A bit of an understatement.

"If you ask me, it was a good thing they thought she'd been fired. It could have been a lot worse if she'd gotten in." Zach pulled the plastic bio-waste bag filled with brain-soaked gauze out of the can and tied it closed.

"She might have gotten something we could use. Even if she couldn't get anything we could recreate, I bet if she'd gotten some evidence linking New Biotech to a potential super strain, we could have gotten the feds involved."

"Yeah, maybe." He sounded unconvinced, and distracted by keeping the bio-waste bag as far away from his body as possible as he took it to the bigger waste container destined for the incinerator.

If we'd kept talking, I might have missed it. But the next few seconds of silence was just enough.

"Have you been reading my files?" I asked, trying to keep my voice tone the same.

"Are you talking about the psycho-babble stuff?" He chuckled. "Why in the world would I want to do that?"

"So no, then?"

"Correct, the answer to your question is no. I have not been reading your files."

"I can check, you know." I said it with all the false whimsy I could muster, which wasn't much.

"Check all you want, I've never touched your files." Zach slammed the lid on the bigger bio can. "I don't even know where you keep them on the server."

"The reason I ask," my heart rate jumped a little when I spoke, "is that I never actually mentioned that they told her she was fired. In fact, I specifically left that part out because honestly I was a little embarrassed by it."

"You shouldn't be embarrassed by it. Wasn't your fault."

My heart raced at this point, and I felt my cheeks go flush, the unconscious excitement of catching someone in a lie. "I know that, Zach. The implied question was how did you know about it?"

"About which part?" He rolled the tray of probes into the sterilizer and slammed down the shiny silver door.

"You know what part I'm asking about. How did you know about them saying she'd been fired?"

He turned to me and sighed the way people do when they decide a lie is too hard to maintain. He didn't need to say the words, but I let him anyway.

"Because I programmed her ID card that way." He made eye contact when he said it, silently defending his position that he'd done nothing wrong.

"You deliberately kept her from getting in?" An edge crept into my tone.

"The macro was set up to show her as fired effective the day before whenever she attempted to scan it. Pretty clever, I thought."

"What the hell, Zach?"

"Look, we have a very specific mission here. We don't need to get all sidetracked with trying to do something we just aren't set up to do or, honestly, qualified to do." He crossed his arms, building a wall between us. "We've got a big building filled with psychologists and neurologists. Nobody in here knows viruses. This lab, it isn't set up for cellular work, and I don't want my residency plagued with a giant failure... or for that matter even a success in an unrelated field of…"

"Zach!" I interrupted. "Have you seen Dr. Marshall lately? You've practically crushed the man's will." I knew that wasn't true, but needed to say it anyway.

"I didn't do anything. He got his hopes up chasing something he should have left alone."

"I can't believe you let me fly all the way…"

"If I'd done it any other way you still would have flown down there. This was the least painful possible…"

"Least painful for you."

"For everyone. This way we'll stay focused and everyone will succeed with what we started. Everybody wins."

"Unless your name is Sigourney."

"She was already dead, Eve."

I screamed at him and stormed out.

When I got back to my room my chest hurt, and I threw myself down on my bed with all my clothes on and stayed there arguing with myself about whether or not I should tell Dr. Marshall what I knew. I finally fell asleep around 3 a.m.

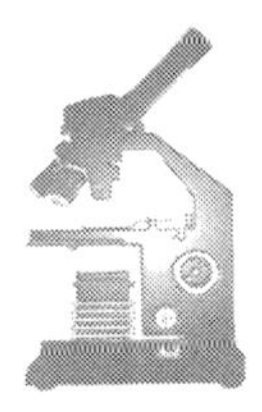

Day 95

Case Study "Ricky"

Interview #19

(Resident Eve Notes: Zach and I weren't talking. We kept to our jobs, but separately. Meanwhile, with Zach and me busy preparing everything for the public group therapy session, Dr. Marshall conducted this interview alone with Ricky. He recorded it though, so I included the transcript.)

Dr. M: "Hello, Ricky."

Hey Clyde, what's up?

Dr. M: "I wanted to run a few routine tests on you today, and thought it might be interesting to chat while I was doing it."

Like I was a regular patient.

Dr. M: "Never hurts to hone my social interaction skills just like everyone else."

Except usually your patients aren't hoping you'll lean too far over so they can bite open your jugular.

Dr. M: "Classically, that's true. Tell me, can you feel this?"

Feel what?

Dr. M: "Good, good. Have you spoken to either of the Residents recently?"

I think I might have groaned at Eve yesterday, but nothing through the wires, no.

Dr. M: "You may feel a little sting here."

Doc, I can't feel anything, seriously.

Dr. M: "Alright, go ahead and move the fingers on your left hand for me."

You know zombies can't control their limbs, Clyde. My hands have probably been straining to throttle you since you walked in.

Dr. M: "Just try for me once."

Sure. There. Anything happen?

Dr. M: "No, nothing at all."

Does anything ever happen with these tests?

Dr. M: "Not so far."

Why did you ask about the Residents?

Dr. M: "We weren't able to get into New Biotech. I wasn't sure if you knew already or not."

You can't say I didn't warn you.

Dr. M: "And tell me, what are your thoughts on us not being able to get in?"

Why would I have thoughts?

Dr. M: "Surely you must have an opinion one way or the other."

Why is that? You think I care about something I can't do anything about?

Dr. M: "Do you?"

If you have the super strain of the virus I'm still dead. If you don't – feel that lack of heartbeat? Sense the absence of breathing? That's me, and I'm still just as dead.

Dr. M: "And that's all you have to say about it?"

Yes, Clyde, that's all I have to say about it.

Dr. M: "Do you think it's possible that you might actually care about what happens to some of the, sheeple, I believe was your word?"

What gave you that idea?

Dr. M: "You were relatively cooperative when we asked you about the vaccine. Tried to warn us against a standard entry, as I recall."

It was an idiotic idea.

Dr. M: "For that matter, you haven't had to speak at all, and yet you keep doing it. You even get frustrated at the mental issues of others."

I've always been frustrated with stupidity.

Dr. M: "I think you know more than you let on, and I think you enjoy the power that comes with keeping secrets."

What secrets?

Dr. M: "But at the same time, I think you're also hoping we'll figure those secrets out and change things, even if it is too late for you."

If you say so, Clyde. Are we done here?

Dr. M: "Yes. All done. And Ricky, thanks for everything."

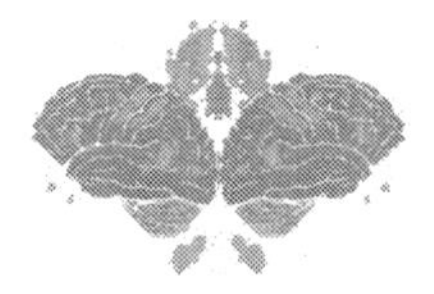

Day 99

Case Study "Dead Man's Party"

July 4th

(Resident Eve Notes: With the loss of Sigourney, the group dynamic deteriorated into a collective depression. I'd decided that the newest information about Zach deliberately foiling the oil rig mission would only cause more harm to Dr. Marshall's mental health, so I kept it to myself. After Dr. Marshall gave me permission to tell the subjects what time of the year it was, subject "Janis" requested she be able to perform her title song for the group. Since she had made her name, literally and professionally, from this song, Dr. Marshall decided it couldn't hurt the morale of the team, and might give us some insights to both how well Reanimates retain higher artistic skills as well as how others respond to music and humor. Zach brought in his grill and Dr. Marshall barbecued some brisket for the three of us. In honor of Sigourney we left it medium rare. Then we hooked the rest of the team together and piped in the appropriate Karaoke music to accompany Janis. The performance was a success, both with the undead and the living members of the team. The recordings sparked mild media interest, and as I understand it, there have been several "Oldies" stations around the country requesting

copies for whenever they broadcast music between tactical updates.)

Janis: Are we ready to go?

Several others: Yeah.

Janis: Alright, let's do this.

Trampled flat in Baton Rouge, tryin to grab a brain
And I's feeling near as faded as my skin.
Zombie grabbed a diesel down before it could escape,
It dragged us all the way to New Orlins.

I pulled the harpoon out of my bloody wet pectorals,
I was clawing walls while Zombie bit and chewed.
Ripping two-by-fours of pine, Zombie's dismembered hand in mine,
We ate every piece of that driver dude

Undead's just another word for no time left to live,
Undead don't mean nothing honey if it ain't me, now now.
And feeling dead was easy, Lord, walking without shoes,
You know feeling dead was good enough for me,
Good enough for me and my Zombie McGee.

From the Kentucky morgue slabs to the California sun,
Hey, Zombie walked and ate without a soul.
Through all kinds of weather, 'cept winter in the north,
Where Zombie baby froze up in the cold.

One day up near the suburbs, he stumbled off away

He's looking for his arm and I hope he finds it,

But I'd trade my rigor mortis for one single working brain

To be finding someone's body free to dine.

Undead's just another word for no time left to live,
Undead don't mean nothing honey if it ain't me, now now.
And feeling dead was easy, Lord, walking without shoes,
You know feeling dead was good enough for me,
Good enough for me and my Zombie McGee.

Argh Argh Argh, Argh Argh Argh Argh, Argh Argh Argh, Argh Argh Argh Argh
Argh Argh Argh Argh Argh Zombie McGee.
Argh Argh Argh Argh Argh, Argh Argh Argh Argh Argh
Argh Argh Argh Argh Argh, Zombie McGee, Argh.

Argh Argh Argh, Argh Argh Argh Argh Argh Argh,
Argh Argh Argh Argh Argh Argh Argh Argh Argh, ain`t no bump on my Zombie McGee yeah.
Na na na na na na na na, na na na na na na na na na na
Hey now Zombie now, Zombie McGee, yeah.

Lord, I'm calling my Zombie, my shambling man,
I said I'm calling my Zombie just the best I can,
C'mon, hey now Zombie yeah, hey now Zombie McGee, yeah,
Lordy Lordy Lordy Lordy Lordy Lordy Lordy Lord
Hey, hey, hey, Zombie McGee, Lord!

Yeah! Whew!

Lordy Lordy Lordy Lordy Lordy Lordy Lordy Lord
Hey, hey, hey, Zombie McGee!!!

Dr. M: "That was very nice, Janis. Everyone give Janis a… well, let's all thank Janis now."

(Resident Eve Notes: Several minutes of thanks and compliments passed from most of the rest of the team. The energy of the entire group seemed to have spiked.)

Ricky: Dr. Marshall, can I ask you a quick question?

Dr. M: "Sure, Ricky, go ahead."

Ricky: Is there any reason you HAVE to disconnect us tonight? Sure, we really screwed up that Dayroom thing – that was my fault, I admit that – but I'd like to think you've disabled all those passwords by now, so we can't really do any harm. I mean, we're all prisoners in our own heads. Most barely even have bodies, and those that do have little to no control over them.

Couldn't we stay linked together tonight, you know, and just talk?

Lisa: Yeah! It will be like a sleepover!

Ricky: I wasn't suggesting we all braid each other's hair and call other boys we like and hang up, but yes.

Dr. M: "We have another group therapy tomorrow, and this one, as you know, is going to have other doctors present. I'd like everyone to be rested."

Ricky: Doc, we don't sleep. Ever. Most of us don't have eyes and if we did we couldn't close them if you paid us.

Dead Eddie: Old Gray… I mean Ricky's got you there.

(Resident Eve Notes: Dr. Marshall consulted with Zach and me, and we, particularly I, agreed it might do the group some good to have another go at some regular social interaction, or at least as much as they were able. I hoped this might be just the sort of moment Ricky needed to come into his own, so to speak. Surrounded by others where he could freely be the Alpha again, but without the temptation to do any real mischief as he had with the Dayroom incident, my analysis anticipated that he would eventually take up the role of protector of them as well. As much as he mocks people who follow him, I think it is a symptom of a co-dependant relationship. He needs people to need him, and this might be the opportunity for him to work towards that goal. With all that in mind, my arguments convinced Dr. Marshall, and he granted their request to remain hooked together for one trial night. Also at my request, given the need to have them interact as people, and not animal test subjects, we elected to make recording optional for the entire evening. I would not have been surprised if they had disabled the recording immediately, reasoning that they must be starved for any semblance of privacy.)

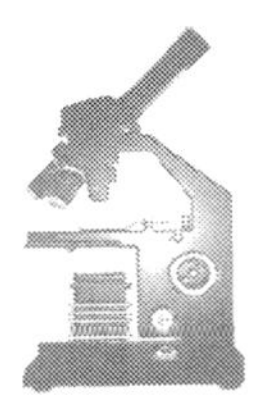

Day 99

Case Study "Overnight Social"

(Resident Eve Notes: While I catalogued this recording data immediately, with everything going on with the public group session, I didn't have a chance to review it until several days later. Ironically, I think if we had just played this candid moment back for the open scientific forum the next day instead of doing the session live, everything would have ended up significantly different for everyone involved.)

Lisa: Well, here we are again. One big semi-happy group.

Janis: Oh boy.

Ricky: It does make one yearn for the good old days.

Sam: What good old days?

Ricky: You know. I haven't had a nice piece of person since… let me think… ah, last really solid gorging I had were these two South Korean businessmen from one of our suppliers. Found them both cowering in a broom closet. Man! Good times.

Janis: Sam, do you remember our last one together?

Sam: That roadie from Queens?

Janis: You *do* remember!

Sam: Like it was yesterday.

Lisa: My last one was yesterday.

Jonathan: What? How?

Lisa: One of the night shift grad students had some scabs from some car accident he was in. I talked him in to peeling those off and feeding me some of those.

Marie: You are *such* a skank!

Lisa: Jealous?

Marie: No, I am not jealous.

Lisa: Jeeeal-lous…

Marie: I am not.

Ricky: What about you, Eddie?

Dead Eddie: Who cares about me? Tell us more about your kills.

Ricky: We want to hear about you, Eddie. What's the last feast of human flesh you remember?

Dead Eddie: Nyah, really, you go next.

Lisa: Tell us, Eddie.

Dead Eddie: No, no.

Ricky: You have eaten someone, haven't you, Eddie?

Dead Eddie: I don't want to talk about it, is all.

Ricky: Have you eaten someone?

Lisa: Answer the question.

Dead Eddie: Dr. Marshall says I don't have to talk about anything I don't want to.

Janis: Answer the question!

Lisa: Answer the question!

Sam: Just answer the question, Eddie!

Dead Eddie: Okay! Okay! NO! I've never done it!

(Resident Eve Notes: Approximately a minute of silence followed Dead Eddie's exclamation.)

Lisa: It's kind of a double-edged sword, isn't it? I mean, if you say yes, you're a murderer, but if you say no, you're not much of a zombie.

Dead Eddie: It was just, everyone around me was already turned. I never got the chance, that's all.

Lisa: I didn't really get scabs from a grad student yesterday. I'm also sort of a compulsive liar.

Marie: Lying skank.

Ricky: Hey, Eddie, don't worry about it. I think it is important you came clean with us. I mean, there is no point in any of us pretending to be something we're not.

Dead Eddie: You mean it?

Ricky: Yeah.

Sam: Good point, Ricky.

Ricky: In fact, I think I'll lead off.

Sam: What do you mean?

Ricky: My name is Ricky. I am not only a zombie, I'm also an asshole. I am an asshole zombie. Before I died, I liked to drive expensive gas guzzling foreign convertibles and I sometimes I deliberately drove slow in the left lane just to watch the expressions of the people behind me. Now that I'm undead, I like a little gallbladder for breakfast. And you know why gallbladder? Because it's hard to find a gallbladder! No other reason. I'm selfish, but my needs are important. I'm not going to be ashamed of what I want or who I am any more! I'm proud of who I am inside, and being dead doesn't change that!

Dead Eddie: Yeah!

Janis: Rock on.

Ricky: C'mon, who's next? Let's hear from somebody else. Hey, Jonathan, what about you?

Jonathan: We all know what I am by now.

Ricky: But we want to hear you say it.

Jonathan: I don't see the point.

Ricky: Jonathan, c'mon. Would you do it if Sigourney was here?

Jonathan: I suppose.

Ricky: Okay, so?

Jonathan: Well. I'm… I guess I am a… a Rean…

Ricky: C'mon, Jonathan.

Lisa: You can do it.

(Resident Eve Notes: Jonathan's readout recorded a large amount of mental activity at this point, mostly jumbled.)

Sam: C'mon, buddy.

Jonathan: I am a *ZOMBIE*!

Ricky: Nicely done, Jonathan!

(Resident Eve Notes: The mood of almost everyone in the group shot up at this point.)

Lisa: I am a zombie slut!

Ricky: Way to go, Lisa! Who else?

Richelle: I am a zombie scientist...

Ricky: Good, Richelle. Next?

Sam: Janis and I, we're not just a couple of zombies. We're a zombie couple.

Ricky: Excellent, and what does that mean to you?

Sam: It means we share things… Everything.

Janis: Awwww.

Ricky: Bravo, Sam! Bravo! Eddie, let's hear from you.

Dead Eddie: I'm just a zombie. And apparently not a very good one.

Ricky: You're not just a zombie, Eddie.

Lisa: No, Eddie.

Ricky: Weren't you a sergeant or something?

Dead Eddie: Master sergeant, yeah.

Ricky: And do master sergeants just blindly follow the mob, Eddie?

Dead Eddie: Well no, they don't.

Ricky: So what's different about you, Eddie? Is a zombie all you want to be?

Dead Eddie: No. No! I'm a zombie soldier!

Ricky: There you go.

Dead Eddie: I'm… I'm zombie strong!

Ricky: Now you've got it.

Dead Eddie: I'm a horde of one!

Ricky: Nice, Eddie, nice! Let me see your war face!

Dead Eddie: Grrrrrrr aaarrrrgh!

Ricky: Wow! Okay, rest a bit Eddie. And Marie, here's your chance.

Marie: What do you mean? I told you, I'm being tested.

Ricky: Tested by whom, Marie?

Marie: Well, I'd like to think that's obvious.

Ricky: Who put you in this situation, Marie?

Marie: What?

Ricky: Who choose to take a big bite out of Bob the Bloated Buffet?

Janis: Nice alliteration.

Sam: Be quiet, he's rolling.

Marie: I suppose I did.

Ricky: Say it.

Marie: I choose to take a bite out of Bob.

Ricky: And therefore?

Marie: I'm being tested by… I'm testing myself. I am testing, *myself.*

Ricky: Faaaaan-tastic!

Tom: I'm Tom, and I'm…

Ricky: That's great, Tom.

Tom: But I…

Ricky: Doesn't everyone feel better about themselves now?!? Huh? Didn't that feel good to get all that out?

Sam: Are we embracing our inner zombie?

Ricky: I think if Sigourney were here right now, she'd be proud of us all.

Jonathan: Here, here!

Ricky: And as much as we all miss her, you know who is really hurting right now? You know who has really taken the loss of Sigourney the worst?

Janis: Dr. Marshall?

Ricky: That's right, Janis, Dr. Marshall. And after all the progress we've made, especially here tonight, I think we owe it to him to try to cheer him up. It's our time to give back.

Sam: He has been pretty stressed about this group session tomorrow.

Ricky: Sam, I think you may be on to something. I think he's worried we're all going to be all rigid and boring, and all his scientist friends are going to be disappointed.

Lisa: Are we going to do another show?

Ricky: No, this is going to be live. I think we'll need to think of something else. Something that will really stick with them.

Lisa: A surprise?

Ricky: Yeah, why not? We'll give them a surprise.

Janis: Should we turn off the recorders then?

Ricky: Good idea. Stop recording.

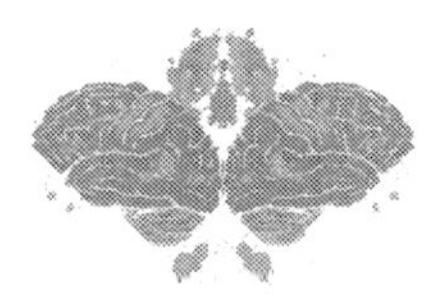

Day 100

Case Study "Group Therapy #4"

(Resident Eve Notes: Once news of our previous successes got out, psychologists, neurologists, and necrologists showed up by the busload to watch the next run. Given the prohibited restrictions of modifying the cleanroom, we instead sent the audio and visual feeds to the building's auditorium. Seating was prioritized by an internal panel, with the seven money people set on the front row center. All the requests for media access were denied. That was Ph.D. Resident Zach's idea. He pointed out that from a public relations point of view, this would get the message of our work out to the world, like a movie preview, without revealing too many specifics. "Building a buzz," as he called it. As an added detail, we set up a microphone in the auditorium to record the reactions and questions of our peers. We started recording the session after the primary introductions, and began with a single primary monitor showing only Dr. Marshall's face.)

Dr. M: "First of all, I'd like to welcome you all to this demonstration we've arranged for you today. I know for many of us travel is a stressful, if not outright dangerous endeavor, and I appreciate the time and effort you've all expended to get here."

(Resident Eve Notes: A few members of the audience nodded, but none made any appreciable noise.)

Dr. M: "As most of you know from our primary papers, we here have made a major breakthrough in the field of Necrotizing Ambulation Disorder research. Before now, there were exactly zero treatises on the human mind's transformation as part of reanimation, other than some basic biological dissertations on cell counts, oxygen levels, and chemical composition.

As a neurologist and a psychiatrist, I felt the prospect of stopping the exploration there was impossible. I founded the NAD Psychological Laboratory Facility with the intent to dig deeper in these victims of Athena's disease. Instead of writing them off as gone, I wanted to hear what they had to say, as I'm sure many others did as well. At last, here, that option is a reality.

We now have the ability not only to read the emotions of the subjects, but also to communicate with them. We can speak with them, listen to them, even provide therapy to help them cope with their condition.

The subjects you see before you now..."

(Resident Eve Notes: Here we turned on the secondary monitor to reveal a wide shot of the entire room and the nine viable subjects. While Sigourney's case studies are amazing, we all thought it best to leave her out of this demonstration given her current condition. The set up had the primary monitor staying on Dr. Marshall. The secondary monitor would default to a shot of the room, and then cut to close ups (triggered automatically)

of any of the subjects as they spoke. The audience, as to be expected, straightened up a little with the shot of the group and the apparatus we use to decode their thoughts, but again, remained quiet.)

Dr. M: "...have spent the last three months going through tests, and verbal interviews, with me and my staff. I am now going to take you through a sample group therapy session like the test runs we've already documented. This is intended less as an exercise in psychotherapy, and more to present the potential these subjects have for recovery. We also hope to show the mental and emotional depths of these NAD sufferers, so long ignored by the public, the media, and sadly, the scientific community at large. In the way of house rules, please keep all extraneous noise to a minimum. Thank you."

(Resident Eve Notes: On Dr. Marshall's cue, we opened all the signal feeds in our standard group therapy session set up. As usual, the group received images of Dr. Marshall when he spoke, and each other as they replied. These same visuals were also sent to the Auditorium for the audience.)

Dr. M: "We will begin today with a simple round of questions from the group, focusing primarily on historical concerns for each subject, as well as observing their potential for social interaction."

Lisa: Is this the part where we talk?

(Resident Eve Notes: A collective murmur from the auditorium piped in at that point and interfered with the decoder. We

reemphasized the need for the audience to remain perfectly quiet except to ask critical questions. It took them a few minutes to settle down, but once completed, we began again.)

Dr. M: "Who would like to share something with the group?"

Ricky: I suppose I could go first.

Dr. M: "Very good, Ricky."

Dr. W, from the Auditorium: "Unbelievable."

(Resident Eve Notes: Dr. Marshall acknowledged the comment from the speakers but also gestured for continued silence.)

Ricky: I'd like to say how much I appreciate all the time we spend together. You and the Residents. I feel like we've gotten a lot closer since this whole thing started.

Janis: Me, too.

Dead Eddie: And me.

Dr. M: "Thank you, Ricky, I think through our talks we've learned quite a bit."

Ricky: Right, yes, sure, our "talks" have been great.

(Resident Eve Notes: I pointed out the abnormality on the screens and Dr. Marshall nodded.)

Dr. M: "Ricky, the decoder actually put an unusual emphasis on the word 'talks,' why do you think that was?"

Ricky: Doc, you told me not to bring that up today. You said they wouldn't be able to tell.

Dr. M: "I'm not sure what you mean."

Ricky: Well, you know, about our time together, just you and me.

Dr. M: "This is a safe place Ricky, you can talk about anything you want."

Ricky: Even the times when, you know, we did, stuff?

Dr. M: "Ricky, I'm not sure where you are going with this, but if you're implying…"

Lisa: No way, you too?!? I thought he just did those things with me!

Dead Eddie: Are you kidding me? All of us? Oh I feel so dirty, so used…

Dr. Q, from the Auditorium: "Dr Marshall, perhaps we should terminate this session now…"

Tom: I thought I was the only one!

Ricky: You said you loved me!

Unidentified voice from the Auditorium: "Good Lord! He's an Undead Head!"

Another unidentified voice from the Auditorium: "Ridiculous!"

Another unidentified voice from the Auditorium: "It's gotta be a joke, people!"

Ricky: Bad touch! Bad touch!

Unidentified voice from the Auditorium: "How could they make this up? They're ZOMBIES!!"

Most of the subjects: Baaaaaad toooooouch! Baaaaaad toooooouch!

(Resident Eve Notes: Dr. Marshall looked around, completely disoriented, until finally he rubbed his eyes and spoke.)

Dr. M: "Stop the session."

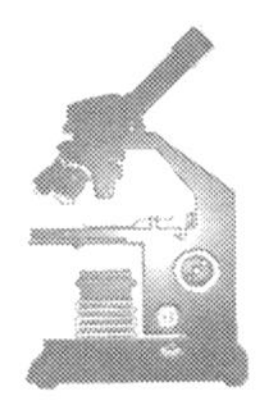

Day 100

(Resident Eve Notes: The auditorium emptied quickly, as to be expected, following the team's outbursts. While Dr. Marshall sent Resident Zach and me to do damage control, we reconfigured the lab back for individual interviews. In the meantime, after only a handful of impromptu discussions we learned that Ricky had coordinated that series of sexual accusations, and that most of the team thought it was a marvelous prank to help make the public session "more memorable" and to both cheer up and help Dr. Marshall. After hearing those comments, Dr. Marshall kept his thoughts on the ramifications of that stunt to himself.)

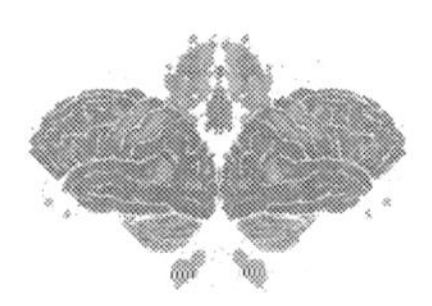

Day 101

(Resident Eve Notes: This morning almost every doctor who attended the event yesterday sent us either a message of support or one of damnation, and the split was far from 50-50. Somehow Resident Zach managed to keep the story out of the immediate media, although he said it was a temporary fix, and they would eventually find out. When that finally happened we anticipated a complete shutdown of our activities and a formal investigation. About mid-morning today, Dr. Marshall called me into his office today for what I assumed would be more discussion on how to recover from yesterday's disaster. As usual, I decided later to transcribe my recordings into prose form again, both as a coping method for myself and a way to organize it for others, particularly in light of what happened immediately after this conversation.)

I opened with, "I don't think it will be as bad as it looked yesterday."

"Well," Dr. Marshall replied, "it could hardly be worse."

His office, ironically, was one of the smallest in the building. I had asked him about it my first week here, and he claimed that the real workers needed more space, and that his office should be the lab, not some desk.

"Is there something else you needed me to do?" I asked, because he hadn't looked up at me yet, which was odd for him. Eye contact was one his strongest features. When Dr. Marshall talked to you, you really felt like he was listening. Sometimes like you were the only person in the room, even if it was a group discussion. This time, though, he focused on his computer screen, which irritated me even more since it was turned away from me so I couldn't see what held his attention.

"You know, before I got into this field, my mentor once told me that the great secret to psychology was that there was no great secret to psychology. It was a very young science, if you could even call it that, and mostly guess work."

"Sir." I don't know why I called him sir in a situation like this one. I did that with a lot of people. "We're doing a lot of good here. The subjects appreciate you. You know that."

"They turned on me, Eve."

"Most of them thought it was a harmless joke. In fact, possibly all of them."

"I know, I know." His eyes still hadn't left the screen. "Cognitively, I'm convinced you are correct, but emotionally, I still feel betrayed. What would you say that was a symptom of, if I were a patient?"

"I couldn't possibly determine after one or two sentences…"

"I wasn't asking you for a differential, just to identify a symptom."

I sighed, not sure where he was going with that. "Do you think you need counseling, sir?"

"It's so easy," he continued, "to think you're immune, facing it from this side. Blame it on stress, that sort of thing." He chuckled and glanced at me for a moment before turning back to the screen. "Even if I'd never accept that answer from one of my patients."

"I have some time free later this afternoon, maybe we should schedule something." I mentally checked my calendar and made a note I might have to cancel a block of time I'd set aside to answer more of our recent "fan" mail.

"I never quite realized the stigma of being on the receiving end of therapy. Having to stand up and admit there might be something wrong."

"And you know that's a perfectly natural reaction," I said. If he wanted counseling, he'd chosen the worst setting for it.

"If no good deed goes unpunished, why do we bother with good deeds in the first place?"

"Is that what you believe?"

"Actually I wonder more about my whole motivation now. Was I ever really trying to help these people, or was this entirely to advance my own career? Maybe it was just for the attention…"

I decided to skip a few steps and go straight to the source. I stood up, pretending to crack my back, which I figured would never pass as natural if he were looking at me, but would do just fine in his peripheral vision. Then I stepped towards the edge of his desk where I could almost see the screen. Since he didn't tense up or try to hide anything I mentally sighed in relief that he wasn't surfing porn.

"You know there is no cause and effect between the work we've done here and what happened yesterday." I kept moving, slowly but steadily. Eventually I could make out the image. Dr. Marshall had apparently hooked up a camera to Sigourney's closet and kept a live feed there. Sigourney looked exactly the same as when she had first been admitted. To me, anyway.

"I'm not sure that's true," he said, finally turning towards me. I couldn't tell if he turned because I was behind him, or because I'd finally seen the screen. "They put on that act because Ricky told them to. Ricky got access to the group because he asked for it, and I granted it. I think there is a very clear chain of behavior there."

"You granted it at my insistence and besides, Ricky's problems are Ricky's problems, not yours. You know that too."

"I suppose you're right." He sounded unconvinced.

"We can't stop what we're doing here."

"No, no, never suggested that." Again, unconvinced. "Although, that assumes we have a choice."

"Why the link to Sigourney?" I figured he didn't need me dwelling on any potential financial problems in the near future, particularly since he knew the money situation far better than I did.

"When she first came in – when any of them first came in – they appeared to be mindless beasts. We spoke to them, got to know them, learned about their true inner being, so to speak." He waved at the screen. "And now, when I look at the most noble of the group, now truly all I see is a beast. Sigourney is gone. Her good deeds, mostly selfless, over years of work, were punished utterly and completely."

"No one punished her. She did this to herself."

"But the means existed to save her, or at least save part of her. Her core."

"We did everything we could." We being everyone but Zach, who had deliberately sabotaged the effort to protect his own career. I strained to shift my emotions from useless anger aimed at my peer towards remaining empathetic towards Dr. Marshall

Dr. Marshall's eyes glazed over for a moment and then he quickly shook his head a few times.

"Of course, of course." He smiled and sounded nearly normal. "I'll see when I can schedule something and send it to your calendar." He stood, indicating we were done.

"Okay, well, thanks for this," I said. "I look forward to hearing more from you soon."

He nodded.

"Really, I think you and I should schedule something," I said.

He smiled and gestured towards the door.

After I left I did a few loops around the building to walk off some nervous energy. I wondered for a little bit about what I would do if the lab closed down. There were other labs, of course, but even with our incredible success, the reputation forming of the group would make landing another research position difficult. I might end up forced to do bag-and-tag work, which tended to rule out worrying about retirement. Worse yet, I might end up working for someone who had been in the auditorium yesterday, and who believed, if even a tiny bit, that our work here, or our founder, lacked credibility.

The third lap around the building I noticed Zach sitting in one of the rooms set aside for more generic biological tests and evaluations. I watched through the window of one door through the window of another door, so I know he didn't see me, and saw him flirting with one of the new graduate students. She seemed polite, but uninterested, and he seemed oblivious. That in and of itself gave me some solace, but the idea that he had the emotional and mental bandwidth to flirt, to even think along those lines, left me standing there clenching my fists. He truly did not care about Dr. Marshall beyond how their relationship advanced his career. It dawned on me then that some of the "paperwork" I'd seen Zach with earlier bore a striking resemblance to a medical résumé; I just hadn't made the connection at the time. He was already hedging his bets, preparing other job opportunities in case everything went south. At that moment I admit I saw him more as a fiend than anything, any *one*, we had back in the lab.

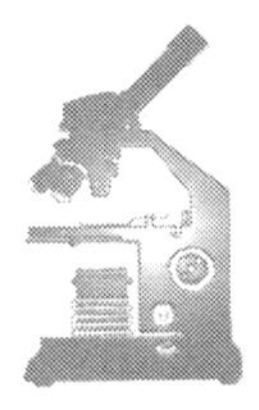

Day 104

(Resident Eve Notes: Several things happened today, and I believe for continuity's sake I will replay the two biggest ones as they happened. To the best of my ability I've been able to sync them up correctly. I will leave my comments in this format so as not to confuse them with the other events, although when my voice appeared on microphone, I will show it as it would normally appear on a transcript.

Dr. Marshall scheduled one meeting with me two days ago, and rescheduled for yesterday, which he rescheduled for today. He obviously knows on some level I recognize he's avoiding me. This implies he either doesn't care, or he just isn't ready to confront what's going on with him right now. When I went into his office today, he hadn't even bothered to leave me a note for another reschedule.

A little perturbed by this behavior, I felt justified in logging into his computer [we all share passwords] and checking his calendar to see what had taken priority over our appointment today. Of all things, he'd slotted another interview with Ricky, and this one apparently a solo session based on a lack of an invite list.)

Case Study "Ricky"

Interview #23

(Resident Eve Notes: This interview was pulled entirely from recordings)

Ricky: How's it hangin', Clyde?

Dr. M: "Let's get right to it, Ricky. You of all of them must realize what is going to happen after our last session, correct?"

Ricky: Golly, nothing bad I hope.

Dr. M: "I know you did that on purpose. You told the others it was for my benefit, but you knew better. You wanted to ruin the one thing that you perceive I have going in my life."

Ricky: Am I going to need to call my lawyer?

Dr. M: "Call him all you want. Would you like to use my phone?"

Ricky: Very funny. Okay, get on with it.

(Resident Eve Notes: While sitting at Dr. Marshall's desk, knowing he wouldn't be done with his interview for awhile, I went ahead and skimmed through his computer. While technically unethical, I admit I let my feelings for Dr. Marshall cloud

my judgment. Hoping for some insight into his latest behavior, I browsed through his Internet history log.)

Dr. M: "All right. You've repeatedly brought up that you believe you can still make a difference in the world, even in your current state. Let's talk about that."

Ricky: Sure. People call us mindless, which obviously this conversation disproves. Sure it's mostly a ride with you in the backseat, but every now and then, if, say, all else being equal, if there is some punk young upstart Vice President and the sweet secretary you hooked up with at the Christmas party last year, and they are both in arm's reach… well then, if you concentrate, the beast gives you a choice…

Dr. M: "You're saying there are times you actually have some control over who you destroy? How would you use that control to change the world? How does that change whether we should be hunting you down and killing you?"

Ricky: You should be thanking us. Who did we get rid of? The slow, the weak, and the stupid. The really, really stupid. A little herd thinning, a little Clorox in the gene pool, everybody wins.

You OWE us. We did you a favor. Just look at the world now. Before we came along everyone was screaming about overpopulation, global warming. Now what are you down to, a couple billion? We got rid of all the idiots who didn't know how to do anything but breed. I mean, seriously, how many of these people we eat do you really miss? The mouth breather at the check out line at Walmart? That kid who kept riding his bike through your flowerbed? There should be a monument to me. The Tomb Of The Unknown Zombie. We eat these morons so you don't have to.

Dr. M: "You ate my grandmother."

Ricky: That's "you" as in "one of you zombies."

Dr. M: "Yes. Not you specifically, just one of you, you ate my grandmother."

Ricky: Oh, come on, she was obviously old. Wasn't she becoming a burden? Wasn't it a little bit of a relief? Because deep down in places you don't like me talking about, you WANT me eating those people, you NEED me eating those people.

Dr. M: "I'm starting to lose my patience with you, Ricky."

Ricky: You know what, you guys don't deserve us. You don't deserve the gift of us helping keep your population in check. We should be the ones calling the shots, and maybe next time we won't stop at just eating 50% of your numbers.

(Resident Eve Notes: The history log on Dr. Marshall's computer, not surprisingly, showed quite a lot of attention to zombie-related articles, and specifically New Biotech. His focus on finding a cure for Sigourney, even after her loss, spoke of a need for closure that Dr. Marshall probably felt could only be found through the super-strain of the Athena virus. I knew better than to think any of the articles even alluded to the existence of the virus, or any way to replicate or find it.)

Dr. M: "These interviews serve no point. I used to think I could help you. You cannot recover. You are a monster."

Ricky: Hurm, what's that on your breath? Steak tartare for lunch today, Clyde?

Dr. M: "And when I say you are a monster, I mean you have always been a monster. The disease just made it more visible."

Ricky: Fairly radical change in diet. Brisket at the July 4th party, too, if I remember right. You want to talk about that, Doc?

Dr. M: "Not now."

Ricky: You mean not on tape.

Dr. M: "Not with you."

Ricky: That's quite a step up from Caesar Salad, I'm just sayin'.

Dr. M: "I am nothing like you."

Ricky: Physician, heal thyself.

(Resident Eve Notes: When I scanned the one article Dr. Marshall had brought up from several different sources, it seemed

unremarkable to me in every way, void of any useful information, until I caught the clue Dr. Marshall must have noticed as well. Then I thought about what he might do with that information. Cursing loudly, I bolted out of his office and sprinted for the lab.)

Dr. M: "Ricky, if you're implying that at some point I got myself bitten…"

Ricky: You figured it out about me, didn't you? I'm not sure when, but you did.

Dr. M: "Yes I did. It didn't take a lot of research, Ricky. Your file lists you as infected exactly six months before you came in, but that's the default date whenever the initial examiners don't know any better."

Ricky: Ah, the outbreak at New Biotech. It was in the news.

Dr. M: "Two years and three months ago, Ricky. Making you either the longest NAD Stage 2 on official record or…"

Ricky: Yeah, all right After I went all Hannibal Lector on the board of directors, one of the R&D guys shot me full of the new super strain. I don't know what he thought it was going to do, but it didn't make me any less undead. I think I might have shoved him through a plate glass window shortly thereafter. The whole thing is sort of a blur.

(Resident Eve Notes: I burst through the doors here, not bothering with any of the standard cleanroom protective gear. I wanted to shout, "Don't let him bite you!" like something from a dramatic high school play, but instead I scanned the room and then Dr. Marshall's general appearance. He didn't appear to be bleeding anywhere and none of his limbs were near Ricky's mouth. I began rehearsing exactly how I would talk him away from Ricky, or if that failed, how I would cut Dr. Marshall's legs out from under him if one of his arms so much as flinched in Ricky's direction.

As all that happened, Dr. Marshall spun around with a furiously furled brow and told me with a look not to say a damn word.

So I didn't.)

Ricky: Hey, the air changed.

Dr. M: "Yes, let's continue."

Ricky: That's Eve I smell. No mistaking that.

Dr. M: "I'd like to stay on topic, Ricky."

Ricky: So now I guess everybody knows my secret.

Dr. M: "Why keep it a secret, Ricky? Why not just tell us you were a carrier of the super strain?"

(Resident Eve Notes: I got the impression he'd repeated that for my sake, since I'd come in late.)

Dr. M: "Clearly you wanted the world to know, that's why you led that horde to move back and forth over the mass graveyard."

Ricky: I couldn't have "led" them anywh...

Dr. M: "Ricky, I've tested your reflexes for weeks. Your body starts reaching for nearby civilians just as quickly as any other zombie, but many times, in our sessions, your hands relax. Usually when you get particularly into the conversation. You forget to make yourself look like a zombie."

Ricky: So I have a little more control than others. Big deal.

Dr. M: "And so you wanted everyone to know about the mass graveyard, didn't you?"

Ricky: I wanted them to know about the super virus, not know about me. I liked being another rotting half-face in the crowd.

Dr. M: "But New Biotech knew. That's why they attempted that legal paperwork to try to get your body back."

Ricky: Oh, please. The same team of lawyers that fought *Fleischer v. Boyle* to a standstill and you think we couldn't get a simple writ through? We had our worst intern working on it and in spite of everything he nearly still succeeded just based on our reputation.

Dr. M: "You failed on purpose?"

Ricky: I didn't have much time to work it out with Augustus, and I certainly didn't explain my motivations to that guy, but the short of it is, yes. You get served with the paperwork, you feel the time pressure, you go out and do something radical and stupid without really thinking it through before you lose your number one favorite patient.

Although, I guess I didn't need to do that. Sigourney's road to madness would have done the same thing, but I didn't know what sort of timeline she was on.

Dr. M: "It seems highly unlikely you were able to get Augustus to…"

Ricky: To have an intern serve a basic writ? Why not? They have a man on the inside of the zombie hordes, I have a man on the inside of a major corporation.

Dr. M: "What could you possibly offer him?"

Ricky: Other than being able to lead one of the bigger hordes around wherever I wanted?

Dr. M: "That's… that's not…"

Ricky: Not possible for Old Gray Eyes?

(Resident Eve Notes: Dr. Marshall pointedly avoided looking in my direction, almost certainly embarrassed I was hearing any of this. The more they talked, the more Dr. Marshall deflated.)

Dr. M: "You lied to Dead Eddie."

Ricky: I need leaders, C, not followers. Them I have by the hundreds of thousands. Eddie needed to learn how to function on his own.

Dr. M: "You've given me a lot to think about..."

Ricky: Well, doesn't matter. I'm still a lab rat, and you? Won't be too much longer for you.

(Resident Eve Notes: Something in Ricky's voice scared me, and I scanned Dr. Marshall one more time for bandages or bloodstains. Nothing. I could still stop him, and moved closer in case I needed to grab him quickly. Dr. Marshall struggled to ignore my presence.)

Dr. M: "Ricky, I have not been bitten."

(Resident Eve Notes: I thought he might have said that for my benefit as much as Ricky's, but he didn't turn to me when he said it like he would have if he were reassuring me. I noticed my heart rate hadn't slowed at all.)

Ricky: Bachelor scientist, no kids, speeding towards that midlife crisis, right after seeing the selfless, noble Sigourney pass on in front of your eyes. Tragic. If you'd figured it out sooner, you might have been able to save her.

Dr. M: "Go on."

Ricky: And all that with your life work about to be questioned in front of an auditorium full of your peers. But just think what it would have been like to be recognized internationally as the zombie whisperer, your name in all the really important journals… and then you could have followed it up in a year with proof that the virus doesn't have to be fatal...

So the other night, when you asked me if I felt anything, you were taking a blood sample.

Dr. M: "Continue."

Ricky: And you can't test it on animals, the virus just eats lesser developed cerebrums.

Dr. M: "If this vaccine…"

Ricky: I knew it.

(Resident Eve Notes: I gasped involuntarily and covered my mouth in hopes that would somehow erase it. My head went dizzy, and I struggled to control my breathing.)

Dr. M: "If this vaccine works…"

Ricky: Oh, you poor deluded man….That's funny.

Dr. M: "Why is that?"

Ricky: This strain does increase oxygen flow.

Dr. M: "How much do you know about it?"

Ricky: Nothing went on at my company I didn't know about.

Dr. M: "So what do you know about it?"

Ricky: It does keep the brain more functional. Ergo, me.

Dr. M: "But?"

Ricky: You guys made the leap to vaccine all on your own. I never said that.

Dr. M: "I see. More brain activity, enough to give the original brain some control over the zombie body, but not enough to keep the body alive. I'm still going to die."

Ricky: You got it, Doc. In more ways than one. Which I must say makes all this time hooked up to this contraption almost worth it.

I've got enough control over my body that I can decide who lives and who dies, and for some reason, my scent attracts other zombies. Not in a food way, but maybe because their version of the virus recognizes mine as a stronger strain. So yes, I can lead them, C, wherever I want, and if the super strain gets out, we'll have a whole breed of smarter zombies just like me. And lookie there, now you have it, too. Soon you'll be strapped to your very own metal slab right next to mine. Maybe they'll even carve your name in it.

Dr. M: "Well then, if all that is true, we have little more to discuss."

Resident E: "You… you bastards."

(Resident Eve Notes: I'd meant to make that last word singular, but I hated them both at that moment. I hated everything about them. My visions clouded a little, and feeling nauseated, I slammed the cleanroom door open and stumbled out to a bench in the hallway.)

Ricky: She took that well.

Dr. M: "Leave her out of this."

Ricky: Nobody knows but her and me, Clyde, and she's not going to go telling anyone. You could still get out.

Dr. M: "Escape? Flee the lab? To what end?"

Ricky: Keep your friends close and your enemies closer. Outside, you wouldn't be just a wanderer, you would be a leader, Clyde. Like I used to be. But maybe you could do better than me, huh? Think of how you could influence this war. Change the face of the planet.

Dr. M: "I've never been a leader, Ricky. I study. I theorize. I guide."

Ricky: Guiding? That sounds like leading to me, just on a one-on-one level. This is your chance to go global.

I'd even volunteer to help, but I know my time has passed. Right, Clyde?

Dr. M: "No Ricky, I'm not leaving. I promise you I will still be here in the morning."

Ricky: For her, right? Eh, you make me sad, Clyde. Well, hopefully we'll still have plenty to talk about after… you know.

Dr. M: "I'm going to wheel you back into your closet now. Good night, Ricky."

Ricky: Hey Clyde, you wanna hear a joke?

Dr. M: "Not really."

Ricky: C'mon, don't be such a wuss.

Dr. M: "Make it a quick one then."

Ricky: How do you tell the difference between the staff and the inmates at a mental hospital?

Dr. M: "I give up Ricky."

Ricky: The patients get better and leave.

Day 107

(Resident Eve Notes: With less than a week before he turns, we've restrained Dr. Marshall at his request and are reviewing his living will. While he hasn't mentioned at what point he contracted Athena's disease and hasn't officially confirmed whether or not he deliberately injected himself with a sample from Ricky, in retrospect, the gradual change to a more carnivorous diet (particularly using the July 4th party as a chance to "lightly barbecue" brisket), the switch from the use of the term "subjects" to "team members," and the frequent trips to the men's room he attributed to his "advanced aging" should have alerted Ph.D. Resident Zach and myself much earlier. His living will, if validated, requests that the scanners be attached to him before the turning, so that they can capture the actual transition, or at least the moment directly after transition. He has also included a request to interact with a patient to be named later in order to study his own analytical abilities as well as his capability to socially interact with others after death.

That's the clinical side of it. On a more personal note, I'm ultimately responsible for his death and I should have known better. He was right about psychiatrists and therapists thinking they are immune to mental problems, immune to stress. Immune to acting on stupid emotions without regard to consequences. I should have noticed the change in behavior and pulled him out of the lab for a few days, and I didn't. I should have discovered Ricky was a carrier in my earlier research, pulled the blood sample from Ricky myself and sent it off to a lab somewhere. Didn't do that, either. Instead I sat back while the most respected man in the field performed a futile and fatal self-sacrifice. And damn that Zach. If he hadn't sabotaged the attempt to steal a sample just to keep his record untarnished, we could have tested it on Sigourney. We would have had time to think it through. Zach. Condescending little prick.

I actually got out some texts on Skills-Based methods of preventing self-harm to keep me from taking another needle of Ricky blood and jamming it in myself. I realized cognitively that another infected scientist in the world wouldn't solve anything. I also realized, on some level, the lure of Athena's disease as an easy way out, exactly as Ricky described it. Damn him, too. If nothing else, once everything with Dr. Marshall is over, Ricky is going to have an accident that leaves him little more than a brain in a jar, if that. I'm still partial to the head-as-soccer-ball idea. I was pretty good at that sport as a kid.

I will probably destroy these notes once this flurry of emotion passes, but for now this, too, like so many other things today, helps me cope.)

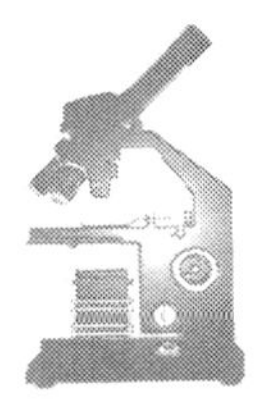

Day 111

Case Study "Dr. Marshall"

(Resident Eve Notes: Ph.D. Resident Zach and I have hooked Dr. Marshall up the scanner to capture the moment of his transformation. We've jury-rigged a special version of the scanner so we could insert the interior probes without causing Dr. Marshall any additional damage, particularly avoiding a brain swelling or a bleed-out scenario. After we have concluded that interview, if Dr. Marshall is able, we will bring in Subject Ricky for a follow-up interview, in order to test Dr. Marshall's mental capacity. In continuation of his ongoing practice of having me describe the physical appearance of his subjects, I shall do so now. Dr. Marshall is strapped in an examination table, still alive, in his lab coat (his request) over a pair of khaki pants and a light blue button up long sleeve shirt. God, it seems so heartless to describe him like the others. Like he's an inanimate object. As expected, he continues to exhibit most of the symptoms of the final sub-stages before "turning." As a point of clarification, all statements from Dr. Marshall before the change are through a microphone hanging near his mouth, and expressed in this document with quotation marks. All statements from Dr. Marshall after the change are through the decoder, and represented in plain text.)

Dr. M: "The room looks a lot different from this point of view."

Resident Z: "It's the lighting."

Dr. M: "I'm sure it is. Not exactly how I imagined my death bed."

Resident E: "Oh sir, I didn't even ask. Is there anyone you wanted me to call?"

Dr. M: "No need. Most of my family is long passed, either naturally or to go off and join the northeastern hordes."

Resident E: "Would you like any more water, or ice cubes or anything?"

Dr. M: "No… No, I…"

(Resident Z Notes: Dr Marshall drifted off for about five minutes, although his vitals remained steady, albeit elevated from his norm. He jolted awake quite suddenly, startling Zach so much he dropped a scalpel.)

Dr. M: "Oh God, I'm dead! I'm dead!"

Resident E: "You're not dead, sir, everything's fine, we're right here with you."

Resident Z: "Temperature up to 102."

Resident E: "It's all going to be okay."

Resident Z: "Blood pressure rising."

Resident E: "Don't you worry."

Dr. M: "Eve! I can hear Zach, okay? I'm a doctor, I'm about to die. I get it."

Resident E: "Yes, sir."

Dr. M: "'Yes sir, you're going to die?' What sort of bedside manner is that? Holy crap, no wonder you work in research… "

Resident E: "Yes, sir."

Dr. M: "Uh, sorry. That might have come out a little harsher than I meant… it… "

(Resident Eve Notes: It was harsher than he meant it. If he'd known how it would sound… how his last words would sound…

Dr. Marshall arrested shortly after his speech trailed off. We were able to resuscitate him for approximately four minutes, at which point he arrested again. We pronounced him approximately six minutes later.)

...a little harsher than I meant it to be...

Resident E: "Hello, Doctor."

Wait, something's different. This isn't just another symptom, is it? It's like looking down a tunnel.

Resident Z: "Welcome back."

Holy cow, you really do smell like dinner and I feel like I haven't eaten in, ever. Not once. Like I've gone my whole life without any food at all. My God, I'm hungry.

And, this is really interesting, on some level I understand my arms are violently attempting to rise up out of these straps to rip you both to pieces, but as far as I can tell I'm not sending any conscious signals to my limbs at all. And I can't really even feel them.

Do I still have my body? You haven't cut off my head yet, have you? I specifically put that in the living will, not to cut off my head until at least one interview.

Resident E: "All in one piece, I'm happy to say."

When I died, I crapped my pants, didn't I?

Resident E: "Sir, I think what we need to focus on now is…"

Oh I did! I did! How utterly humiliating…

Resident Z: "Sir, this is an historic moment."

(Resident Eve Notes: "Historic moment." I wanted to slap him.)

Resident Z: "If you could talk us through how it happened, while it is still fresh on your mind."

Right. And I appreciate you not calling me Doctor Poopy Drawers. Don't think I didn't notice. Back on topic. For one, this machine really gives me the impression I'm just talking, and I really have to concentrate to realize my mouth isn't moving at all, or if it is, it's just trying to snap at one of you. My mouth also seems to have no inherent depth perception on its own since you are both well out of reach.

I think Ricky's analogy about being in the back seat is spot on. All I can do is observe, which sounds like it would be hell, except whatever part of me used to gag a little at the idea of eating part of another living being while they were still living, well, that part is totally gone. In fact I feel like my mouth is watering just being this close to you, like I'm drooling all over myself.

Resident Z: "You actually are drooling all over yourself there, Slick."

Oh, Zach, you're going to taste good when I empty out that brain pan later. JOKE! Don't cut my head off for it.

Resident E: "Sir, if there is nothing else, we can end the interview and go straight to the memory and cognitive function tests."

Okay, yeah, let's do that. Otherwise this is just going to degrade into a bunch of cannibalistic innuendo and then me begging for any excess organs you aren't using. Like your appendix. There's a sweet number you could do without. Take it off your hands, free, no need for the trip down to the bio-waste incinerators.

Sigh, see what I mean? Go ahead. But we need to hurry so there is still time for me to interview Ricky today. That's got to happen today.

Resident E: "Yes, sir. Good to see you in high spirits, sir. Signing off."

(Resident Eve Notes: Zach conducted the tests while I excused myself to the break room where I sobbed like a little girl. I guess there is little else to say about it than that.

From Zach's notes, Dr. Marshall did well on the modified Choice Reaction Test, the Match to Simple Visual Search test, and the Rapid Visual Information Processing test. In all cases he seemed agitated, and wanting to hurry the testing up as quickly as possible. The MRI detected quite a bit of hemosiderin – old hemorrhaged blood – throughout the brain stem, as well as a marked decrease in the insulation jackets around the axons of the frontal lobes. Other than that, Dr. Marshall seemed like a

normal healthy undead doctor. With him, at least, in a relatively upbeat mood, we moved on to his next request.

I knew then that this would be my last moment to hear Dr. Marshall's voice. Everything ended that day. All our work, all our research, everything we'd done, was about to wrap. I backed up all our files on the remote servers and set this interview to save itself there as well. One way or another, I was done.)

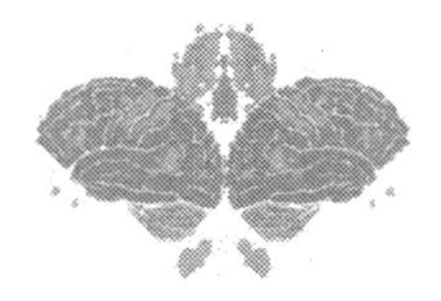

Day 111

Case Study "Dr. Marshall" and "Ricky"

(Resident Eve Notes: We completed Dr. Marshall's transformation interview approximately two hours ago. While Dr. Marshall's body remained on the examination table, I wheeled in Ricky on his mobile cart and attached the two together through the decoder. After a few other adjustments, I asked Dr. Marshall if it was okay if Zach facilitated the interview while I waited in the observation room. I said I'd been monopolizing the interviews and Zach was going to need to step up once he was gone. I think what everyone thought was that I just couldn't handle it. That was partially true.)

Dr. Marshall: An interesting side note is that when all the probes are in that I can actually 'hear' my own voice through the return loop. We did this better than I thought.

Resident Z: "Yeah, I do good work. Sure you want to go through with this? I haven't powered Ricky up yet."

Dr. Marshall: Of course. Despite your doubts about the field of psychology, it is a very delicate science, Zach. It should be very interesting to see what my mental faculties are capable of during this new state of being, as it were.

Resident Z: "If you say so. Still, why interview Ricky? He creeps me out. Sometimes he even looks like he's smiling."

Dr. Marshall: Would you rather a test be easier, or would you like to see limits being pushed?

Resident Z: "Valid point. Powering up now… you're both online."

Dr. Marshall: Hello Ricky.

Ricky: Look at the dead brain on Clyde.

Dr. Marshall: I know this is a little awkward, Ricky, but let's continue as if this were a normal session, shall we?

Ricky: If you say so.

Resident Z: "All righty doctor, are you feeling okay? Is there anything we can do to make you more comfortable before we begin?"

Dr. Marshall: No no, I don't need any special treatment. Let's just continue like we normally would.

Ricky: Except for the part where you're dead.

Dr. Marshall: Yes, thank you Ricky. Except for that part. How would you like to start us out today?

Ricky: First of all, I'd like to thank you both for this opportunity. Dr. Marshall, I'd like to thank you for agreeing to see me today, and Resident Zachary, is it?

Resident Z: "Most call me Z."

Ricky: Yes, Resident Z – that's funny.

Resident Z: "Hilarious. If we could continue…"

Ricky: Anyway, Z, I'd like to thank you for letting the last person to strap me to this chair be an overly compassionate Ph.D. Resident Eve, who also has a crush on your good Dr. Marshall there.

Resident Z: "What are you…"

Ricky: Whoopsie, that belt was a little loose…

Resident Z: "Oh, shit."

Dr. Marshall: Ricky, would you like to go first? Is there anything you'd like to share with us?

Ricky: At the risk of being cliché', Bbbb-brrraaaaiiiinnnnnssssss....

Dr. Marshall: I see, I see. And what about you, Zach?

Resident Z: "He's biting me! Oh, Jesus, God, he's biting me! Christ, it hurts! Get him off! Get him off!!"

Dr. Marshall: I see, and how does that make you feel?

(Final Resident Eve Notes: The equipment failed after those words, presumably because the internal contacts were either ripped out of the subjects or out of the apparatus. To clarify, at the first sign of trouble I tripped the alarm and headed for the Safe Room, stopping briefly along the way to grab Dr. Marshall's autographed hard copy of **Undead Like Me.** ***I made it, along with 3 others, and we remained there for two weeks until rescue personnel signaled us with the correct code and voice recognition to open the door. Prior to that, we had a rather disturbing moment later the same afternoon as the accident. Someone entered the correct code, but couldn't produce anything audible that the voice recognition software could identify. I can only hope, truly, truly hope, it was a malfunction.***

Most of the rest of the lab occupants simply ran for their lives. To date, two of the employees have been spotted in a newer northern horde, and the bodies of three others, including

Ph.D. Resident Zach Smithee, were recovered on the grounds either with their brains removed or with their bodies too mangled to be mobile after they turned. While the body of Sigourney was destroyed in the small clean room fire, neither Ricky, Dr. Marshall, nor any of the other subjects have been seen since.

As of the publishing of this document, all study of NAD -afflicted personnel has been put on indefinite hold, and I've taken a sabbatical from research. Lab research, anyway.

I admit I blamed Zach for Dr. Marshall's death. I still do. If Zach had helped more to get the super-strain, gotten it where we could have examined it instead of Dr. Marshall testing it on himself… And I also confess, then, to Zach's murder. I hardly think it will matter except to whomever finds these pages years after I'm long gone. As a record keeper, I wanted to keep the facts straight to the end.

I want the world to know that I thought it through before I did it, although a part of it was impulse, true. Dr. Marshall, such an original and powerful mind, twitching on a slab. I just couldn't stand to see him that way knowing that Zach was next in line to be the head of the lab. To imagine Zach running the research, to visualize him in charge of the institute Dr. Marshall worked so hard to create, it always came down to the more likely option of Zach driving the entire program into the ground through apathy and incompetence.

But again, I did think it through. We had Level Three lockdown procedures. It should have been a quick mauling followed by a brief investigation, some cursory questions, and back to business as usual, sans Zach. Escape should have been impossible… unless one of the zombies got help from someone who helped write the protocols, designed the building, knew the codes... So by letting Ricky loose on Zach, I also released him into the world, and he took Dr. Marshall with him.

I don't know if they are working together. I also don't know if Ricky found a way to infect the other subjects with the super-strain or if they just followed him out. All of them but Sigourney. I guess she was too… well, I guess she's not useful to them anymore.

I will miss the group, the interview subjects I came to know, and I will mourn for each. Knowing their thoughts, their feelings, now warped and twisted under Ricky's lead...

I'm still angry at Dr. Marshall. He, like Marie and Sigourney, he gave up. No matter what else happens, I will never let someone near me do that again if I can help it.

And given all the pent-up rage I'm now feeling, I'm set on joining a militia somewhere. As Lola put it, no matter what they were before, on the outside they are still rabid animals. All except Ricky. Of all of them, he is the only monster. Maybe my insights will help the defense forces before Ricky can do too much damage. I have an old friend from school in charge of a paramilitary group up in Fargo, and hopefully they could use someone with my skill sets. And maybe, if I'm lucky, if I have to train on every weapon and learn how to track his footsteps from one coast to the other, maybe I'll get to make a soccer ball out of Ricky's head someday after all.

Session Terminated.

-- Resident Eve L.)

-- End of Report pursuant To I.S. Res. 257, 123rd Cong., 5th Sess. --

Made in the USA
Charleston, SC
13 June 2011